HIS VIKING QUEEN

CAT CAVENDISH

MARIE COLE

His Viking Queen

Cat Cavendish & Marie Cole

This is a work of fiction. Names, characters, businesses, places, events and incidents are either the products of the author's imagination or used in a fictitious manner. Any resemblance to actual persons, living or dead, or actual events is purely coincidental.

Fans of Ashe Barker, Kathryn Le Veque and Emma Prince are in for a new sexy Viking treat!
A fierce alpha warrior, Bjarke Marsson, was not ready for what the Gods had in store for him. One terrible raid on their village and he found himself in a position of power and duty and with a new wife. He shouldered the responsibility of caring for his people with honor, but the one thing he wished for himself was forbidden - his shieldmaiden.

Dalla Koridottir, married three times, widowed three times, an orphan and a shieldmaiden, was used to being an outcast. She knew her place — a distant admirer of the fierce warrior, Bjarke. Never had she imagined that he would desire her or work so hard at trying to claim her for his own. His duty to his people and her fear of letting another man into her life are almost enough to keep them apart.

With war on the horizon and a promise laying in his bed Bjarke struggles to keep Dalla out of his arms and his heart. Will this Viking warrior be able to convince his shieldmaiden that his love is true? Or will the curse of the Raven tear them apart?

Author's Note: *This book contains very sensual scenes with a dominant alpha male that some may find borderline consensual. If you are sensitive to dominant men then please do not purchase this book.*

CHAPTER 1

SPRING

743 A.D.

The soothing sound of the water breaking on the shore washed over Bjarke who was still tense from a heavy battle. The sea grass tickled his face on either side as the wind blew. The sunlight warmed his naked, freshly washed skin. His tanned flesh gleamed with many scars that revealed his many trials of battle throughout his twenty seven winters. His seafoam colored eyes peered into the sky above and he wondered what was transpiring this moment in Valhalla. The raid for gold and treasures had been a lucrative one, but a great number of men had given their lives for it.

He closed his eyes again as he reflected on one in particular, his brother, Fleinn. Bjarke stared into the sky where Odin and the rest of the Gods lived – Valhalla, the magnificent colossal hall where fallen warriors, only those worthy, retired after their existence in this world was over.

"You fought well brother. I will see you soon enough in Valhalla and there we will drink until we burst with mead."

For a moment his eyes shimmered with tears but the rustle of meadow made his hands shift to wipe them clear.

Dalla's shield fell down onto his face before he had a chance to take in her strong but feminine naked body as it headed towards the water. "Do not weep for Fleinn. He died with honor." She was a shieldmaiden and had fought alongside him since they both were old enough for battle. She was likewise a widow three times over and, allegedly, barren if the rumors around the village were to be believed, leaving her less than desirable in other men's eyes. Bjarke himself had never considered taking a wife. The village was full of women more than amenable to spread their thighs for him. And he had no need for one, he would not be jarl, leader of his village, that was his brother Fleinn's place, but now it was left to the second oldest, Sigurd.

Bjarke shook his head to relieve the force of the blow. He clambered from the ground and peered at her backside as it retreated into the water. "I know he died with honor, but that is not why I grieve." He didn't stare as moved towards the water to follow her.

"Why then, does the almighty Bjarke Marsson cry?" Her hair, black as the raven's feathers, was now floating around her. In battle she wore it back tightly bound in braids, but she had loosened it to bathe. He thought she looked captivating either way, but he knew better than to become tangled up with her. He had been resisting his hunger for her for many winters, even before they started fighting alongside each other. His father, Mar, warned him it was unsound to lie with your shieldmaiden lest she grow angry with you and move away from your guard on the battlefield when you might need her the most. But as Bjarke gazed at the crystalline water lapping at her milky skin he prayed his father had been mistaken. He knew a good roll around in the grass would make him forget for a little while the grief and loss he was suffering from the death of his brother.

Bjarke waded into the water, his chest and torso muscles rippling as he moved. His dirty blond hair was cut at chin level and upon his face was a considerably thick beard where a narrow braid dangled at the chin halfway down his chest.

"Because we will not be able to go whoring together anymore." He sloshed water at Dalla who barely blinked as the water forcefully hit her face.

"That is, indeed, much to cry about." She splashed him in return before migrating further away from him. Did she move elsewhere because she desired him also? Or did she turn away because he repulsed her? She was difficult to gauge. She was not a commonplace woman who fussed and fawned, craving male attention. She was a shieldmaiden, robust and unflappable, and praises to the Gods, so remarkably beautiful, unlike any maiden in his village. None had the blackness of hair like she bore.

Bjarke admired her body as he mopped his face with his hands and slicked his hair backward. She didn't twist around, but she must have sensed his eyes on her back.

"Can a warrior not bathe in peace?" She melted beneath the water and later resurfaced again, further away. When she smoothed back her own hair her latest battle wound could be observed. It was at least half a foot long, deep and a furious shade of crimson.

He grimaced as he glared at her wound, untended, as if it were a mere nick of the blade. He realized she had suffered it while defending him. If she had not been behind him, that nasty gash would have landed on his back and he may have fallen along side his brother.

He didn't understand why she cared so little for herself and it irritated him. "You should have cleaned your wound. You are lucky a sickness has not also grown in it," he observed as he glared at her.

She hastily put her arm down, as if embarrassed that he'd caught sight of it. "My wound is no concern of yours, Bjarke." She swung away then and commenced walking further away through the water.

He growled, his chest vibrating as he proceeded through the water towards her. "It is of my concern. Get out of the water and go visit the healer or I will drag you out like the insubordinate child you are being."

"Touch me and I will make certain the blow meant for your back finds its mark, Bjarke." She stopped walking away and shifted around to stare him down, her fists hidden in the water along with most of the rest of her. Only her head, her shoulders and the absolute top of her generous bosom showed.

Bjarke clinched the muscles of his jaw. Dalla was lucky that she was such an exceptional warrior or he would not be as tolerant. Nonetheless she needed to be taught a lesson about who was in charge, just as she would if she were a man under his charge. Not only was he the Jarl's son, he was also the one in charge of the raid. "Such a threat from someone with an injury. Perhaps it is you who will get another." He moved closer still, watching her like a hawk circling a field mouse.

"My sword hand is still in full working order. Would you care to test me?" She withdrew, not from him, but closer to her weapon which was resting amongst the tall grasses on the bank.

A slight smile played along his lips as his eyes tracked her. "I would like to test you." He licked his lips eagerly. He knew it was not what she meant, but she made herself an easy target at times to his sexual teasing. And while he normally controlled his impulses to tease her, he could not resist now even though he realized he should. Anything to take his mind off of the death of his brother.

"Spare that talk for a maiden." She shot back, fury blazing in her grey eyes, the water now retreated to her curvy hips. Her breasts were concealed by her wet hair, which essentially covered her pale erect nipples beneath.

The smirk on Bjarke's face widened as he swallowed his amusement. "Are you not a maiden? You have the most generous breasts. They plead to be teased. And the slit between your legs would no doubt be a wondrous fit."

"I am not a maiden for you, Bjarke Marsson. Do not speak to me of those subjects again or I will take out your tongue and burn it as a sacrifice to Freya."

The water sloshed against his skin as he moved through the water. She stiffened as he advanced closer, but made no step towards her sword. He was not certain if she wished for him to grab her, but presently his mind was entirely centered on calling her bluff. She was such a beguiling woman, and the most alluring and touchable. It made him crave her even more.

He picked her sword up and plunged it into the sand on the shore and settled her shield upon it. He himself drew the two axes from the belt near his clothes before standing at the ready. He had not sparred in weeks and sparring with Dalla would certainly be an amusement. "Pick them up," his voice resounded with authority as he shifted to face her. "Cut my tongue out. It will stop me from licking between your thighs later." He was only partly teasing her. The thought momentarily distracting him as well. He shook it from his head as she came from the water.

Her jaw clenched tight when she placed the shield onto her injured arm, but otherwise seemed unaffected as she readied herself for the fight. She gripped her sword firmly in her grasp as she met his eyes, they twinkled with delight. "Gladly."

CHAPTER 2

Without warning she closed the distance and took a swing at his left ax.

He allowed the blow to match with his ax. Her blade slid up towards his hand, but the right ax came up and seized her blade away from him and forcing it high toward the sky. His knee came up into the shield on her arm to aggravate her injury.

Sweat popped out on her brow and she grunted as she drew her sword back and swiped at his exposed thigh.

He smiled as she did so. He had anticipated it would be her reaction. He locked his axes around her sword and jerked it from her grip. Bjarke pushed himself into her guard and they both went down in the sand with him on top of her. He could not help the erection that was pressed against her thigh. He worked to ignore it and attribute it to the fighting, or the absence of female company since the raid began, but as he stared down into her shocked eyes he was momentarily disoriented. He was so absorbed in the feeling of her soft

7

womanly flesh beneath his that he didn't see her hand until it was too late.

She cupped her hand and brought it to his ear with force.

Bjarke shook his head as he roared out in surprise. A stream of blood slid down the line of his jaw. "I am astounded, Dalla, that you would choose such a cowardly defense against me."

"I am astounded that you were bested by your shieldmaiden."

His luminous eyes crinkled at the corners as his lips drew up into a smirk. "Bested? Is it not I who is on top?"

"Being on top of a mountain does not mean you have bested it. It means the mountain has favored you to partake in the view."

His eyes dipped to her naked form beneath his. Her breathing was ragged, her creamy skin intersected with scars that should have deterred him. And yet in this moment he wished she would let him trace them with his tongue. If he were being forthright with himself his shieldmaiden had been enchanting to him for quite some time. But he'd never acted on it. He never dared to because she was such a great warrior. But this day, this moment, when his brother's life was lost, he allowed himself to get closer. "I have yet to encounter a mountain view as awe-inspiring as this one," he murmured, his head slowly sinking towards hers, his tongue swiping at his lips, wetting them for her.

She did not shy away and yet she whispered, "Bjarke, stop before I inflict death upon you."

His leg advanced and spread her relaxed legs as he slipped between them, his erection finding the warmth there. He chuckled tenderly. "Do you think I fear death?" His lips grazed the tender flesh of her neck. He groaned in appreciation, he had never known skin to taste as sweet as hers. He required nothing more than to make this woman his. He wished to claim her. Possess her. Lose himself within her. The taboo of it, because she was his shieldmaiden, simply drove him desire her more.

She inhaled sharply as one of his hands wandered down the length of her body. She shivered beneath him as his palm cupped her sex, a single finger exploring.

A gasp of pleasure curled in her throat. "Stop, Bjarke. I am your shieldmaiden. I am not your thrall." Her warm fingers came down upon his shoulders, curling against the mounds.

He beamed at her comments that conflicted with every other part of her. Had she not wanted him to be between her legs she would have him on his back in agony. He had watched her do it many times before with various men who thought they were in her favor. "I did not ask you to be my thrall. And I do not want you to forget. But instruct me once more to stop and I will." His finger pressed lightly against her folds, he grunted in satisfaction to discover it was moist with excitement.

Her hips rose to greet his finger, her lips separated and her cheeks glowed as he teased her with his finger. She was stunning.

"Tell me, Dalla," he looked down at her, watching as she answered to his touch.

"Bjarke..." Her nails sank into his shoulders. Her hips fell as he pulled back.

He curled his fist, his finger glistening with her arousal, and set it on the earth beside her. "Aye?"

She opened her eyes when he drew away, her face a blend of

dissatisfaction and annoyance. "Is this but a sport for you, Bjarke? Am I nothing but a con—" She clipped her words when she heard male voices approaching and shoved him with all of her strength. "Get off, now!"

Bjarke rolled off of her and onto the grass with a grin on his handsome war-scarred face. He admired her naked body as she seized her things. She shielded herself as the other warriors passed to have their turn in the water.

Sokki, a fellow warrior and one of Bjarke's oldest friends, regarded Bjarke with a not so subtle grin. "Did we ruin your fun, friend?" He chuckled as he, and the other three scarred warriors, stripped out of their clothes. Bjarke looked over his shoulder and regarded Dalla's naked backside.

Bjarke grumbled as he got up from the ground, the opportunity to savor her further wasted. He took both his axes and headed for his clothes.

One of the men watched Dalla start to dress herself as he spoke. "What good is a woman who cannot have offspring?"

"Good enough to amuse men around the campfire," the other one shot back with a loud laugh, "too bad that one does not partake in such things. I found out from Bersi's own lips that she was the best he ever had."

"Of course it was the death of him," another replied. The outbreak of laughter echoed across the water.

Bjarke's jaw clenched as he struggled to overlook their ignorant words. The death of Bersi, Dalla's third husband, had been hasty and many moons past, but it was nevertheless a subject of considerable gossip in the village. He ached to defend Dalla but he would not lest his secret desires of her become known. If word of his intentions were delivered to his father it would be the end of raiding with Dalla at his side. Dalla "The Black Widow" would not be suited to be a Jarl's wife and his father would see to it that his legacy would be preserved. Not that Bjarke had any intention of being Jarl. He had at least one other older brother who would receive the title before him.

Sokki came close to Bjarke and draped an arm around his shoulders, leaning in close so the others couldn't overhear him. He spoke into the non-bloodied ear. "Can you hear anything other than a loud ringing? Do I need to go with you to see the Jarl, your father?"

Bjarke gave a vehement shake of his head. "I hear fine from the other. I can speak for myself when addressing my father," he replied gruffly as he bent over to pull his pants on and then his furs before turning and heading towards the ships, leaving them behind to gossip like idle maidens about Dalla and her infamous venomous nether region. It would be another week or so before they arrived back in their village with their riches, and until then he had to be sure Dalla stayed far away from him. She was too tempting by half.

CHAPTER 3

They arrived in the village one week later. As the ships landed at the dock the villagers cheered for the return of their warriors. Most of the villagers were in their fields, planting their crops. The women, some at home tending to their children and chores, were most striking as Bjarke stepped onto the wooden platform, erected many summers ago by him and his four brothers.

One of Bjarke's long-time companions, Astri, sighted him and waved from her spot beside a weaver's tent. She leaned down to convey something to her son, Engli, her breasts nearly tumbling out of her top, and then stood up and headed towards him, her hands innocently clasped behind her back. "Welcome home, Bjarke." Her blue eyes raking over his appearance, as if soaking it into her memory.

His eyes shifted to her as he held the guise of no emotion on his face. "The jarl will demand to see me. It will be my neck if he waits too long."

"After visiting the jarl I will come meet you. After the sun has kissed the sea." She placed her palms on his chest as she stepped in front of him, her head tipped back, expecting a kiss.

Bjarke seized a handful of her hair and tugged her head back further before peering down at her tits which were on display for him. They were only mildly appealing after having Dalla's pressed against his chest and that annoyed him thoroughly for Dalla was off limits.

"If you have forgotten it is I who will come find you if I crave your company."

He roughly thrust her aside and heard her gasp with shock. He caught sight of Engli gawking at him, the young boy's fists clenched tight aside his eight year old body which was already larger than average. There was no mistaking that he had Marsson blood in him. But it was nevertheless unclear whether it was Bjarke's or his brother Fleinn's seed who had created the bastard boy. Bjarke had slept with many women and only this child had the possibility of being his. His brother Fleinn, on the other hand, had fathered many and Bjarke doubted after observing many who could have been twins with Engli that he could be the father. It was unfortunate that all offspring of Fleinn would now rest on his father and his older brother, Sigurd's shoulders. They would not allow a child of theirs go hungry. Fleinn had done well at populating the maiden's tents with his seed.

Bjarke ignored the boy's bitter gaze as he crossed towards the center of the village where the hub of all political and social activities took place. The Great Hall was where the jarl, the head of the village held his place at the end of the seemingly infinite rows of wooden tables. He and his wife sat there and listened to grievances, issued orders and recounted stories. It was their duty to make certain the people under their care thrived.

Once inside the Great Hall Bjarke moved through the vast crowd of people who were assembled around the fire in the middle of the considerable building. He still only heard through one ear, the ringing in his other was becoming annoying, a persistent reminder of what had transpired between him and his shieldmaiden. He pushed Dalla from his thoughts as he halted at the foot of the raised chair which seated the jarl, Bjarke's father.

"Bjarke, welcome home." The jarl promulgated, loudly enough for all to hear. The man was almost as well-built as his son. The only contrasts between them were the color of their eyes; Bjake's eyes had taken the blue seas of his mother while the jarl had the dark piercing eyes of a crow. The jarl's hair was longer, braided neatly down his battle scarred back.

"Jarl. Father," Bjarke said as he stared the older man in the eyes which held the same shape of his own.

The jarl's tone was now marked with only a tinge of heartache. "We have already received news of your brother, Fleinn. Tonight we do not mourn for him for we know where he is." The jarl came down from his post and clasped Bjarke on both his shoulders and gave him a single forceful shake. "This night we celebrate! You led your warriors well, son. This night we feast for the survivors and sacrifice for good fortune. I choose you to give the praise to the Gods."

Bjarke's jaw jerked as nodded his head, working to let go of the discomfort that he was holding onto as his thoughts shifted to his fallen brother. He had led well, but not well enough to spare lives. "As you wish, Father."

The jarl smiled. "Good. After you and your men are rested

you will raid again. We have received rumors that Jarl Torg from south across the sea wishes to lay claim to our lands for his fields have become barren. I expect it best we go to him before he reaches us, and let him know, in no uncertain terms, that this is our land of Asar and it belongs to us."

Bjarke's head bent forward in respect, as was expected of him, and any other citizen in their village. "Of course. My axes are yours."

The jarl nodded his head in approval. "Go. Rest. We will speak more of it later." The jarl clapped Bjarke's shoulder once before turning his head towards his wife who was still perched next to his place at the head table.

Bjarke observed his father move towards his mother. Her blue eyes were soggy with tears. Bjarke would have preferred to comfort her, but he knew he would be reprimanded if he'd done so. She was the jarl's wife and as such she had to remain strong.

Bjarke fled the Great Hall, in no mood to boast of his accomplishments, and drifted past the people of the town, walking along the wooden planks downed side by side to create walking paths. He passed the markets, and the Seer's longhouse to the water's edge behind his own longhouse, where he could be, for a moment, in peace.

He stepped around his canoe and wandered out into the water, the bottoms of his breeches darkening with the sea. The ocean was still cold this early in the season. Bjarke plunged his hands into the water and let the chilly salt water coat his face as his hands ran over it and through his hair.

"Bjarke!"

His head whipped around when he heard a sweet little voice

behind him. When he shifted a little girl waded into the water at him. His lips quirked at the corners as he took in her gangly limbs. His little sister, his only sister, was growing so fast.

"Kerra." He hoisted her in his arms and pecked her brow. "You have seen seven summers now. You are growing old like me."

She giggled and brought her slender arms around his neck. She adored her older brothers and tended to follow them around whenever they were home, which was never often enough. "I cannot wait to be old like you. I wish to be a great Shieldmaiden and fight with my old brothers." She beamed as she brushed her forehead to his.

"One day," he replied with a proud grin. "One day you will." He stepped from the water with her and sat her down on the beach. "Go back to the village center and play with the other children. I will see you this night at the feast. Perhaps you can aid me in giving blood to the Gods."

"Swear it to the Gods?" she asked, excitedly, bouncing a little. It was not often the village would let a child engage in the sacrifices. The privilege and responsibility was usually given to an older member, someone who had earned it, respected it, and had proven themselves worthy.

"I swear it, little one," he insisted her as he put his hand on her blond head.

"Wait until I tell Fleinn! He will be so pleased!" Apparently news had not yet been shared with his sister regarding Fleinn's death. It was likely his mother's duty and she would have been too distraught to say the words.

Before he could explain she dashed off. A scowl marred his

face. Tonight she would find out. Tonight she would learn of her brother's death and how the honor it. Bjarke's heart was heavy as he left the water and made his way into his long-house which was indistinguishable amongst the many others that sat in long lines across from one another. The jarl's son, once grown, did not receive special treatment where housing was concerned. His longhouse was created from lumber, mud and thatch, just like everyone else's. He did not have jewel encrusted walls or fancy gold adornments.

He nudged aside the bear skin that kept the cold from stealing his fire's warmth and abandoned his axes near the entrance. When he peered down the length of his home he felt no surprise as he saw Astri laying on his pallet. The woman was insistent, if nothing else, and wrapped up only in his furs. She did not say anything, instead slowly moved a fur, displaying half of her delicate, velvety skin.

Bjarke allowed his eyes travel over her body as his hands worked on the strings of his pants and unfastened them. She was not Dalla, but perhaps if he spilled his seed he would stop thinking of her.

"I told you I would come find you," he replied, his voice gravely and laced with slight irritation. She knew him well enough to know when she should speak. This was not one of those times. She casually drew the other side of the fur to the side, fully exposing herself to him. Her face remained uncommitted.

His pants fell to the floor as he shifted closer. He was starting to show some excitement. He lowered himself to the furs as his hand slid between her legs.

She was already wet, it coated his fingers as he shifted them between her slit. She arched her back and held tightly to the fur on either side of her head.

Bjarke moved between her legs and drew his fingers out of her. His powerful hands seized hold of her and lifted her after rolling her onto her stomach so she was on her knees. There was no time wasted as he pressed against her and started to drive in.

"Do you not prefer to look at me?" Astri peered at him over her shoulder.

"Shut up," he grumbled. He thrust himself deep inside her making her cry out. Before he could close his eyes and envision a dark haired woman beneath him he noticed small jolts of pain along his backside. He pulled out and stood to see Astri's boy, Engli, settled by his front door, resentful, a large jagged rock in his right hand, poised in Bjarke's direction.

"Leave my mother alone!"

Bjarke growled and reached out for the boy but before he could snag him, he rushed through the doorway and out onto the public walkways.

CHAPTER 4

"Help! Help!" Engli sobbed as he ran. He was panting wildly, fear made his eyes crazy. "Help!"

Dalla's brow wrinkled with concern as the boy ran towards her. She seized him by the shoulder with her good arm, he struggled, but once he was still she knelt down and peered into his petrified gaze. "What is all this commotion for?"

Engli pointed towards Bjarke's quarters. Her eyes followed, and she wondered what Bjarke had suggested to the boy to make him so frightened. This boy was his blood after all. One of Fleinn's many bastard sons.

Dalla sighed as she rose. She hastily moved Engli behind her and stepped closer to a group of women for concealment as Bjarke stormed out of his house, searching in both directions for his offender as he hurriedly retied his pants.

Astri ran out behind him clinging to a fur as she stared at his backside. "Do not hurt the boy!" She clutched onto his arm.

19

Dalla's heart thumped wildly as she set eyes on Astri. Perhaps it was not Fleinn's son after all. She had not realized that Bjarke was lying with Astri as well.

Bjarke jerked his arm away from Astri, who freed him almost immediately and brought her hands to her lips. Dalla reached behind her and clutched Engli's hand. Turning, she knelt down, and she spoke quietly so she was not overheard, "You should not poke the bear, boy. It is honorable to protect your mother, but it is not your fight. Not yet. Not until you are old enough to protect yourself. Do you hear me? Run now, that way, so he does not find you. Come back to your mother's home after dark. Go." She encouraged him towards the woods and again glanced back to Astri and Bjarke.

Bjarke turned on Astri. "Do not hurt the boy? I would not kill blood without cause. He is the spitting image of my brother at that age and he has Fleinn's dislike for me as well." His hand took hold of the furs and tugged her closer. "But I am not my brother. You will do well to remember that. He was the nice one. In his honor I will provide food for the two of you, but beyond that..." His jaw twitched with ire. "Keep that boy and yourself away from me." He jerked the fur from her body, leaving her standing in the pathway between the long-houses naked.

Astri scrambled to enter again but her clothes came flying out, halting her as they struck her in the face. She snatched them up and quickly fled before her shame burned her from the public humiliation.

Dalla pressed her lips together firmly as she urged her feet to move in the direction of Bjarke's home. She believed herself lucky that the men had snuck up on them when they had or she might be the one naked outside his home. But even as that thought crossed her mind she knew that it was not in Bjarke's nature to publicly degrade women. Despite the meaning of his name—Bear—he was not brutal and cruel unless he were facing an enemy. Something was not right, and she was going to find out what it was.

She paused at his doorway, not wishing to be on the receiving end of his anger. Not unless the anger was flamed by her to begin with. But her desire to help him overpowered her fear. "Bjarke?"

The flap opened slightly. She noticed his eyes glance towards her arm and they moved elsewhere when he was satisfied that she had cared for it. "Dalla," he boomed, the fury still evident in his voice.

She peered around outside, taking in the curious faces turned in their direction, before looking back to him. "Are you alright?" she asked quietly, taking in his rigid stance, his labored breathing.

"Tonight should have been my brother's night to lead the sacrifice, not mine. It was my command that led my brother to die for us. How do you think I feel?"

"It was not you who killed him." She glanced around once more before stepping past him into his home. "Are you going to cry again?" she asked, her head bent as she advanced towards his fire which, as all others did, lay in a circle of stones in the middle of his house.

"If you have come here to poke fun at me, then you can leave."

She raised her head and spun around fully to look at him, there was no judgement or humor on her face. "I did not."

She swallowed hard and shrugged her shoulders as she recognized that he was sad. And she recognized what might take his mind off it if even for a little while. If rumors amongst the maidens in the village were to be trusted, he was quite good at it too. "Perhaps whoring is what you need. To take your mind off it."

His eyes had been cast towards the fire until she spoke. Those sea foam colored eyes fixated on her now and she felt her heart hammering in her chest. A man never made her feel the way he did, not any of her three husbands, may they lie around with full bellies with the Gods. With just a gaze Bjarke could make her flood and fill with an indescribable energy. She usually did not know whether she wished to run from him or towards him. But he was Bjarke: the jarl's third oldest son, and she was not but an orphaned runaway. She'd been widowed thrice, and she was a barren shieldmaiden.

Despite how he was regarding her, his eyes making promises of pleasure and satiating a need, she did not want him to ever mistake her for a carefree woman because she was not. She could not give that part of herself to him, she was his shieldmaiden. And when it came time for him to marry, it would destroy her to be cast aside, or worse yet to be asked to be his kept woman. She had no false hopes that she would ever be anything more than an average person in the village, one of the rest. She was not special, and she knew she never would be.

She glared at him to discourage him and shook her head, holding up her good arm to keep him from advancing towards her. "I did not mean myself. You have a village full of women. Do not look at me that way."

His eyes glanced away from her and to the fire and for a

moment she felt sadness that his attention was no longer on her.

"There are. Ten of those women have bastards from my brother," he confessed.

"Why are you so sure they are your brother's? Aside from the hair on your head and a few more wrinkles on his brow, you looked as if you could have been twins."

"Because I cannot have children. The Seer, the one who sees all, told me this. And even if he is not to be believed I have only lain with one of those ten. All ten bore him children. I have lain with many women and none have birthed my seed," his words came out in a strangled whisper.

"No one would know they are not yours, Bjarke. They are still blood," she said it equally softly, "Astri would make a pleasant wife."

Bjarke scoffed at her suggestion, the regret and sadness in him gone, replaced with indignation. "Why should I choose a wife? There is no need for one. I will not wed until I need to when the village requires a jarl's wife to be at my side. And it is known that Sigurd will now be the next jarl."

"What about for love?" Dalla asked, regretting the words almost instantly. If Bjarke thought for a moment that she had womanly feelings for him she would be doomed. And so would he. For everyone in the village knew what happened to the men unfortunate enough to request her to marry him.

"I would marry for love. But I do not love."

"Of course. A fine warrior as yourself would be destroyed if he chose to love someone."

"Love is not a choice," he said, "or is it? Did you love your husbands? Or were they merely between your thighs for your protection?" His eyes shifted back to her and she felt her cheeks start to heat.

"I did not need them for protection!"

The low call of a horn signaled that the celebration was about to start. She released her gaze and moved towards the doorway of his home.

"Did you not?" His hand grabbed her good arm and his grip tighten.

She stopped because she had no choice. She was in no condition to fight him. She needed to heal before the next raid or be left in the village to be bored nearly to death with menial tasks that other women partook in, like weaving, childcare, cooking. But she did not want to argue with Bjarke. Not about this. And she needed to distance herself from him before he discovered what she was craving in that moment more than fighting. "The celebration is starting. You will be missed." It was the only leverage she had, and she did not hesitate to use it.

Suddenly she was pressed against the wall, her body pinned by his mass. She felt his lips on hers, demanding a kiss. She groaned, letting her body get lost in the feel of his lips on hers. For a moment she forgot everything but him, the smell and the taste of him. And then she remembered Astri and how she did not want to be cast aside again. She bit his lower lip, her hands on his chest, trying to push him back.

The horn sounded again.

He broke the kiss and stepped back, leaving her surprised and perplexed by his behavior.

"You needed protection from me, Dalla," he proclaimed as he licked his lower lip. He grinned at the blood he tasted and Dalla felt her insides clench in excitement. He was right and if he continued to pursue her like he had been she was in trouble.

CHAPTER 5

Dalla pulled Catrin aside roughly as soon as she entered the Great Hall where most of the village gathered for the evening as they invariably did after a party returned from a raid or trade.

"Ow! Dalla, you brute! What has gotten into you?" Catrin observed her friend carefully as she rubbed her arm where Dalla's fingers had imprinted on her fair skin.

"Cat, I think he wants me."

Dalla had no one else to tell her secrets to, Catrin was as much as a sister to her as she could hope for. It was Catrin's parents who had found Dalla at the wood's edge when Dalla had been but nine seasons old, broken and bruised, fleeing from her dark past. It was Catrin's parents who had married Dalla first after Dalla refused to help with the chores in the household, preferring instead to fight with the boys.

"Who wants you?" Catrin looked around, most of the men were too busy with their mead and their maidens to notice the two of them gossiping. But one warrior had his eyes fastened to Dalla and when Catrin spotted him she glanced back to Dalla, her lips twisted up in a grin. "Bjarke? You could do worse, Dalla. I have already mentioned to you how impressive he is." She winked and lightly nudged Dalla with her elbow.

She didn't want the mental impression of Catrin and Bjarke lying together. Or his member, which she already learned was unusually impressive because not that many moons ago he had it pressed like a threatening sword between her thighs.

Dalla yanked Catrin's arm to shut her up. "Stop that," she scolded and Catrin lost most of her grin. "He is misguided. He is seeking a woman to lie with and you and I both realize it will not be me."

"Dalla, there are times in life you must take a risk. Do you not think he is worth it?" Both their eyes shifted to Bjarke who was still staring at Dalla, his fingers idly stroking the braid at the base of his chin. Dalla licked her lips, the recollection of his lips on hers forcing their way back into her head. Bjarke leaned forward, smirking, but before he could make her any more uncomfortable, the jarl pulled Bjarke aside, drawing his attention elsewhere.

"You are not asking the right question, Catrin. This is not about Bjarke's worth. It is about mine. I am worth more than that." She raised her chin defiantly. "Bjarke will discover that I will not bend to his will sooner or later. He will not own my body without also giving me his hand in marriage and I will not accept that from him. We are doomed. I will never again shed tears over a husband's grave. Is three times not enough for any woman?"

Catrin grinned as she bit off a generous chunk of meat from

the bone she was holding. "Sounds like a most entertaining game." She snorted in surprise and then giggled as a warrior pulled Catrin into his lap. Dalla watched as her friend flirted and teased the man, a visiting Viking, from where she was not sure, she did know however, that he was a stranger.

Dalla left her friend to flirt, there was nothing more to do about Bjarke, except to drink away any awareness of him. She sat down amongst a few shieldmaidens and generously filled her cup. She drank from it hastily and then filled it again.

"Dalla, a fine warrior is gawking at you," the maiden beside her whispered.

Dalla groaned and without looking up from her cup she replied, "Yes, I am aware. If he knew what was best for him, he would let only his eyes touch me."

The maidens chuckled which caused Dalla to look up. She peered into the eyes of Sokki. He was a handsome man, strong and unattached since his wife perished in childbirth two summers past. The babe did not survive despite the many prayers to Freya.

"Dalla," he replied with a bow and a rather disarming smile.

"Sokki," she acknowledged softly, still uncertain of why he was standing there peering down at her.

He held out his large hand and Dalla looked at it until the maiden beside her poked her elbow into Dalla's side. Dalla laughed to mask the pain she felt and placed her hand in his. She stood and made her way with him towards the rear of the hall, her cup still in hand. "Sokki, is everything alright?"

"I saw you and our jarl's son on the grasses by the water,

Dalla, and I cannot seem to remove it from my mind. Tell me true, do you have affections for Bjarke?"

When she sought to turn her head to look at the offensive face that matched the name Sokki held her chin in his hand, holding her gaze on his. "No, dear Dalla. Do not look at him. Tell me. I spoke with him and it seems he is agitated." She was about to fight him when he freed her. She struggled to quiet her raging nerves. Sokki wasn't trying to harm her, she knew that. Her body, however, was conditioned to tell her something different.

"Of course he is overcome. He has just lost his brother in battle."

"It is more than that. One look at him and everyone in the village of Asar can see that the jarl's son is smitten with you. Do you have affections for him?"

"I have feelings of pity for him."

Sokki whistled quietly. "You pity him?"

"Yes. He is pouting like a child whose wooden play sword was snapped in half. And the truth is that the play sword did not belong to him in the first place."

"Do you have affections for me?"

She was taken off guard. Sokki was handsome, aye, and a fellow widow, but she did not wish him to die due to her curse any more than she wished it upon Bjarke. And even if that were not the reason, he was Bjarke's friend. And given how she felt about Bjarke she would not act on those feelings either. But there were none. "I have feelings of friendship for you."

Sokki grinned as he grasped her cheek between his fingers,

giving it a slight tug back and forth. "And I have feelings of friendship for you as well. You are an exceptional warrior. And full of passion."

She winced as he released her. "You are drunk," she stated with a grin, smoothing her burning cheek.

"Maybe I am," he bragged as he too produced a grin towards her. "Do you tell him?" he inquired.

"Do I tell him what?"

"That there are feelings." His head cocked to the side as he gazed at her, then his head angled to look up at Bjarke.

She followed his gaze. Her eyes fixed on Bjarke, drinking him up as he sat beside the jarl, his father. "No. He is the jarl's son."

Sokki laughed. "Dalla, you are funny. Many women paw at the chance to lay with the jarl's son, many less claim feelings. He is just a man like I am."

"And I am a widow, three times over." Sokki's heavy arm fell down on her shoulders and she grunted.

A twinkling of revelation sparked in his eyes. "Ah, so you do have affections for the jarl's son. You simply hope to spare him from some silly curse. And it is that — silly. Tonight is the night, Dalla. Come," he implored as he worked to urge her to walk closer to the raised table. "Tonight it comes out."

She shook her head as his hand slithered down the length of her arm. "No, Sokki, and you will keep your lips tightly sealed about what I have confessed to you."

She could feel someone staring at her as Sokki kept his hand on her arm. "If you don't go talk to him, then maybe I will, Dalla." His eyes glittered with mirth as his lips perked up into a teasing smile. She turned her head to see Bjarke with his eyes on the two of them. His gaze was practically burning them both.

She turned her gaze back to Sokki. "You tell him and I will cut off your balls." There was a slight twitch on Sokki's lips as he regarded her own humorless smile.

Sokki's tongue swept along his lips as he examined her face. He was judging her seriousness, causing her to frown. That sealed it, he shrugged his shoulders in defeat, "Fine. I will not speak since I am attached to my balls."

She put her hand to his scruffy face and gave it a pat, "Good man. Excellent choice." She drifted back to her seat and sat down once more, the feel of Bjarke's eyes on her back was starting to scorch her. Sokki followed. He leaned away and snatched another flask of ale. His eyes shifted towards Bjarke and then he turned away to move amongst the other warriors.

It was then she noticed Bjarke's sister standing beside her table, a witness to Sokki's minor assault. "Kerra." Dalla bowed her head in respect for the young girl, the jarl's only daughter. "I drink for your brother this day. He is doubtless already drunk with his friends in Valhalla, yes?" Dalla offered Kerra the softest of smiles in case the little girl lost herself to grief.

But she did not, instead the little girl bowed her head, receiving her regards. "He was a great warrior." She shuffled her feet a moment before glancing up and speaking. "Brother wished to see you."

Dalla raised her cup to her lips and pretended to drink when the ale did not meet with her parched lips. It was empty. She didn't wish to appear to be a fool any more than she already was. She swallowed her air mead and then lowered her cup.

31

"Thank you for the message, Kerra. Inform your brother that I do not wish to see him. I have company waiting for me elsewhere."

She shrugged her tiny shoulders. "I will tell him you go to see Sokki then." The little girl bowed her head and scurried away.

Dalla refilled her mead as she watched Kerra make her way to Bjarke. He plucked her up in his strong arms and she leaned in close to tell him her news.

The grin left his face and after a moment he set his sister's feet down beside his seat. He settled his hand upon her head to show his affection and then left his sister standing there as he stood moved off the perch. His long limbs had him striding quickly past many merry villagers and fellow soldiers. He avoided them all, heading for the exit.

Dalla and her cup followed after him swiftly. She hadn't expected him to leave the Great Hall, for it was he who was being honored. When she let Kerra take the message to Bjarke, she had expected she would have time to warn Sokki, but she'd misjudged and now he was going to receive the brunt of Bjarke's rejection.

She followed him as he moved towards Sokki's home. He disappeared into the house and after a few long moments of silence there were sounds of destruction inside. She gasped softly and hid in the shadows when she saw Bjarke emerge. "Where are you?!" His battle cry was full of rage and impatience.

Dalla felt a warm male form behind her and was about to scream when a finger tapped her lips. It was Sokki.

"Shh."

They both watched Bjarke grab a small wagon and obliterate it against the front of Sokki's home, four of the logs holding up the roof collapsed, sending thatch raining down. It was an impressive feat of strength. The muscles of his body bulged and without a person to destroy he took off towards the woods.

Sokki whispered, "Will you let your friend lay with you now? It is possibly my last moon."

"Shh. I am not his. He is being a beast because he has lost his brother. This is not about me. But I will fix it. Fear not. You will live to see many more moons, Sokki. And to lie with many other women."

CHAPTER 6

With three strong cups of mead and no food in her belly she was ready to face her fear. Before she set after him she turned to Sokki.

"Can you deliver a message to Catrin?"

Sokki stared at her in the near-darkness for a moment before lifting his brows in question. Sokki nodded as she pressed her cup into his chest.

"Please tell her that I have left to confront Bjarke and that if I do not return by morning, then she needs to dispatch someone to find me."

Sokki grinned as he grabbed the cup. "I will pass along the message, shieldmaiden. Be careful. I hear the Bear likes to be rough."

Dalla ignored the quivers that ran from her body at his implied sexual innuendo. She twisted away from him and made her way to the woods where Bjarke had disappeared.

Dalla did not fear many things, but the woods at night was

one of them. In her childhood the dreadful things would always happen in the woods. The shadows were never just shadows. And her screams of suffering were never heard.

The moon was mostly full, casting a light everything it could touch through the treetops. She stepped along slowly, seeking to avoid stumbling on roots in her already inebriated and uneasy state. "Bjarke?" she called out, her voice shaking.

She heard the crackling of a fire and observed how the ember's flickering light cast shadows through the trees. It took a moment for her eyes to fixate on him. He was just finishing kneeling before the fire. He crossed to sit on a fallen log by the fire, but he did not speak.

She stepped near him, going around the small fire. Her heart was beating fiercely in her chest. She was ready at any moment to be snatched from behind. She was on alert. She was not comfortable here. Until she glanced across the fire and saw Bjarke. Seeing him made her feel safer. Seeing him she felt that if the man in her nightmares grabbed her, Bjarke would do everything in his power to stop him.

Dalla sat down across the fire from Bjarke in the dried leaves, which were beginning to crumble in the spring warmth. "You should not take your pain out on innocents."

The way the fire glowed on his face made him look like a man possessed. He sat there with his arms on his knees and his knees up to his chest. His eyes glared at her through the fire. "Sokki is no innocent. Why will you lie with him and not with me?" His words were still irritated and yet he sounded as petulant as a young child.

"I am not his shieldmaiden," she said, remaining perfectly still under his gaze. It was the truth, but not the reason.

"Then I will cast you off onto him. And then you can lie with me."

She felt her stomach drop at his remarks. Did he care for her or did he merely wish to conquer what was forbidden to him?

"I am the best shieldmaiden in the village. You wish to compromise that so that you may ravage me? Is it worth that much to you?"

Bjarke held his determined gaze upon her without saying a word for a lengthy moment as his lustful eyes took her in. She felt naked sitting across the fire from him under his scrutinizing gaze. "Come here and sit upon my lap and perhaps I will answer you." He sat back and wiggled his knee.

She felt the shame burn on her face at his reply. He did not care for her. She was simply a conquest, and she had been a fool to expect that it was something else. She blamed the mead for her stupidity at coming after him. She stood up and threw a fistful of dirt upon his fire before stalking away from him, back into the woods, the place she feared. She made it a few steps into the woods before she felt his firm grip on her wrist to stop her. For a moment she felt the panic, but when she rounded and saw him it weakened. But her anger did not. She wrenched her wrist free. "Have you chosen to answer me now?"

"I do not have to answer you, shieldmaiden. You already have the answer to your silly question."

"Aye. You will not rest until you have bed every maiden in the village."

He chuckled as he came closer, caging her in against a tree, his arms mocking being around her as his palms pressed against the coarse bark of the tree. "Nay. There is something about my shieldmaiden that excites me. I cannot see what it is."

Her heart was still scrambling, her nipples strained against her dress at his nearness and the way he looked at her in the darkness. This was very different from the last evening she'd spent in the woods with a male. This was not unwanted. But it was scary, for profoundly different reasons.

"I can," she said, eager to put distance between them lest her body would betray her heart and mind. "A woman says she does not want you and you find it to be a challenge."

He pressed his lips together as he stared at hers and shook his head. "Nay. This may come as a disappointment to you, shieldmaiden, but you are not the first to reject Bjarke."

It was a shock, but she refused to show it.

"And if I thought you meant what you said, shieldmaiden, I would not be here. I would not have destroyed my best friend's home. I would not have tried to lay you in the grass. If I thought you meant it I would be at the jarl's table, where I am supposed to be." His eyes roamed her face, settling on her own eyes.

She swallowed the lump in her throat, her heartbeat had jumped to her ears. She could plainly hear how every word affected her pulse. She was frightened her heart would burst. She opened her mouth to speak but his finger came up to press against her lips. There was tenderness in the touch, but it was clearly a command.

"No. You will only lie. I felt how much you appreciated me between your thighs, Dalla. Tell me the truth, no more lies

37

about fighting the way that you feel for me because you are my shieldmaiden."

She saw her chances at fighting him off quickly slipping away. If she were going to walk away from him with her dignity intact, she was going to have to do exactly as he was accusing her of. She would have to lie. She felt the squeeze in her chest as the words managed to squeeze from her tight throat. "Fleinn promised to marry me. I will not be with a man who is third best."

She felt his hand around her throat and felt the stabbing of the bark of the large tree as it pressed into her back. She closed her eyes against the hurt so clearly expressed on his face. "I do not believe you." His grip was strong around her neck but he did not stop her breathing. It was for show, to try to scare her. But she was not easily scared, especially not by him, for she knew no matter their disagreement he would not harm her, just as he would not truly harm Sokki. She was not Astri or any other of the maidens he used to keep his furs warm. She would not cower to him. And she would not bend to his will unless she wanted it.

She opened her eyes. "You never do." She grabbed his hand, quickly and effectively disabled it, pulling his thumb towards his wrist.

He grunted, and jerked his hand away from her, his thumb dislocating in his haste. As quickly as he'd pressed her against the tree, he'd released her. She heard the growl as he reset the thumb and saw him stalking back towards the fire as if defeated. She held onto the tree behind her for strength.

He sat back down on the fur by the fire and looked into it.

When she looked at Bjarke, she saw not a man but a boy. A boy who was mourning the loss of his brother. A boy who felt responsible for a death he wished he could have prevented. A boy who desperately wanted to be held and comforted. If she were any other maiden in the village, she would have gone to him, held him, and kissed away his grief. But she was not. She was an orphan with a shameful past. Even if she hadn't been barren, the jarl's son should never lie with a woman who was as broken as she.

CHAPTER 7

Yarl Torg stood on the bow of the ship and stared at the torchlights flickering against the inky blue night sky. A smile crept over his lips as he envisioned what was to come in the next few hours. The waves that lapped at the shores of Asar would soon be ripe with his best warriors.

Beckby was a place he no longer wished to call home. His people's crops were not producing, the livestock was growing ill with mysterious symptoms and the women were no longer birthing children. Of the last year's children only two had survived. He did not wish to watch the mothers bury anymore of their babes.

This was the only way and tonight he would strike while he knew that Jarl Mar was drunk and weakened, his son and their warriors just returned from battle. They would be impaired and drunk on an endless supply of mead. It would be straightforward to move under the cover of night and slit many throats.

He did not wish to do it but it was what would need to be

done if the land would be secured for his people. They would not coexist harmoniously. How could they?

"How much longer are we to stand here gawking at this filthy village, Father?"

Torg's jaw clenched. He shifted and glanced over his shoulder to his daughter. Gerd was as beautiful as her mother had been with long copper red hair, pouting heart-shaped lips and cheeks sprinkled with freckles. But she had not acquired her mother's grace, or patience, nor her taste in men.

Of all the men in the village, she'd chosen the one young man different from the others, the least worthy. There was something about the young man that Torg did not like. There was a darkness about him, something sinister. He knew if he forbade his daughter from being with the man that she would run straight into his arms, just like her mother had done with Torg. King Harvard had been furious when his only daughter had fled from Trelleborg to Torg's home of Beckby to marry him. And Torg would not at all be surprised to discover that King Harvard was seeking his revenge for the death of his daughter on the people of Beckby.

King Harvard was too cowardly to fight with his swords. He was growing older and weaker and it would only be a matter of time before a younger, stronger man would rise and strip the crown from him.

Perhaps it would be Torg. Perhaps he could seek his revenge on behalf of his people once they were settled on their new lands.

Torg settled his hands on his daughter's delicate shoulders. "This dirty village will soon belong to us. We will stand here and gawk at it for as long as it takes to ensure victory for our men. I advised you to stay, Gerd, I do not know why you insisted on coming along. The battle will be a bloody one." Torg lifted his eyes to the ship to his left. He had lied to his daughter, he knew precisely why she'd preferred to come along. For the young man who was standing at the rear of the boat like a coward ready to turn tail and run at the first sign of death.

"I will stay on the boat until you come for me, Father, just as you've instructed. And if matters do not go as planned I will return home and tell the others."

Torg nodded and again turned away. The cheers and song from the Great Hall were dying down. Torg was growing anxious, impatient, but he knew rushing this battle could be catastrophic. He would wait.

"Soon, Gerd. Soon our men will invade and kill. Soon this land will be ours."

CHAPTER 8

Dalla was almost to the edge of the village when she heard the warning horns blaring through the evening sky. She smelled smoke and heard shrieks of maidens and young children. She paused just in front of the farthest longhouse from the center of town and gawked at the chaos before her. Her people were fighting everywhere. And those that were not fighting had already perished or soon would. There were fires all around her, nearly every building was lit, casting a hauntingly bright radiance on the battleground that used to be her village. The largest fire was coming from the Great Hall. It was engulfing the building in a large inferno. The furious flames practically licked the sky. Her initial impulse was to fight, she reached for her sword. When she realized it was not there, she knew she should go retrieve Bjarke.

She spun to escape. Suddenly, her world went black from the blow to her skull she hardly registered.

When Dalla peeled her eyes open, her skull was pounding as if someone had slashed it open with an ax. Her vision was so blurred that she could make out shapes of people around her, but no clear faces. Her arms ached in their awkward position behind her. She struggled to free them but her wrists and ankles were bound. She blinked, trying to clear the bells from her ears. The village was in trouble. Bjarke was either bound, or, more likely, dead. Whoever this was invading their lands would not keep him alive if they knew his worth.

Slowly her vision cleared, and she saw faces of others from the village there with her in a broad circle, torches sprung up around them, casting a flickering glow. The fires that had taken most of the buildings were now nothing more than smoking ashes. And blood painted the ground, the moon and torchlight shimmered on the dark liquid pools.

She glared at the man in the middle, the one who seemed to command the most respect. The large blond man with one eye. Jarl Torg. She had heard of him. Everyone had. The legend of how he had lost his eye was no secret. He had married King Harvard's wife without the King's consent and as punishment the King had Torg's eye cut out. He would only see half of his bride, the half he'd tarnished and sullied.

It was likewise no secret in Asar that Jarl Torg wanted their lands. They were fertile, and Asar's access to the larger trading villages to the North easier than Beckby's.

Dalla clenched her jaw tight and pushed herself to focus on getting herself free. She would not submit. She would go to Valhalla tonight if need be to save her brothers and sisters. She slowly turned her head, she didn't want to bring attention to herself, and located a pointed rock a few feet from her.

If she could...

Jarl Torg slowly stepped around the interior of the circle as he spoke. "Your jarl is dead, as is all of his family. Swear an alliance with me and you shall live. You may carry on your lives in Beckby in peace, farming and fishing, undisturbed."

She whipped her eyes towards Jarl Torg, frozen by the confirmation that Bjarke was dead. She peered around again to see if perhaps Bjarke had deceived him, her heart hammering against her ribcage as hope lingered in her chest. But none of the faces were his. The sinking in her chest deepened.

She blinked the tears away as she focused on Sokki who was laying at her feet. His head thrust forward to look in her direction and she saw blood dripping from a substantial cut on his face. One of his eyes was swollen shut. She regarded him as he slowly inched his way towards her.

On the far side of the circle a man managed to stand, even with his bindings. "You are no jarl of mine. You have no honor."

Without hesitation Jarl Torg approached him and silenced the man by thrusting his blade through the man's larynx.

She kept her eyes forward even as she felt the bindings on her ankles and wrists loosen, thanks to Sokki's magical fingers. Jarl Torg killed three more people while Sokki freed her limbs. She was about to spring forward when Sokki hissed. She stilled and glanced over her shoulder at him. He peered up at her, a grin on his swollen lips. He pressed a large pointed rock in her hands. She gripped it tightly, shielding it within her fists.

"Does anyone else wish to die? No? Good. Those who were

too cowardly to stay and face my warriors will be found. They will not be given the same choice."

"Jarl Torg!" Dalla interjected loudly, holding her position on the ground. "Please, let me pledge properly."

Jarl Torg smirked as he sauntered over to her. "You wish to pledge your fealty to me, maiden?"

She peeked up at him, doing her best to play the part of the innocent maiden. She nodded. "On my knees, my jarl, as is proper, please? I wish to pledge so the others may follow suit. I do not wish any more deaths to fall upon my people."

The gasps from other victims that enveloped her were loud.

"How could I deny such a brilliant, beautiful woman the request of wanting to be in front of me, on her knees?"

Jarl Torg nodded to a couple of men who came over and restored her to her knees. They fell back when a couple of women started wailing at her, their voices carrying dirty remarks to her ears. Remarks Dalla knew were untrue. And soon they would know it too.

She bowed her head and waited. Patiently. For the right moment.

His sword picked up some of her hair and let it fall slowly to her shoulder. "Raven's hair. That is not common. Perhaps your mother was a witch. What is your name?"

"Dalla, Jarl Torg."

He waited for the silence to settle around them before inquiring, "Do you swear your allegiance and fealty to me and to my family from this day forth?"

"I do not, Jarl Torg." She regarded the confusion on his face as she stood, ripped her hands free and slammed the pointed rock deep into his good eye. While he roared in pain she seized his sword, and without compassion or extra thought she stepped behind him and slit his throat. She grunted with extra effort as she hacked it from the rest of his body. She held his head up as a threat to his warriors, who gawked at her in awe for the moment.

"He is no longer your Jarl! Leave now and I vow no harm will come to you!" Her face bloodied, she walked deliberately around, slashing the ties that bound the strongest of her fellow villagers. Her poor injured arm was shaking from the weight of the head and the height at which she held it.

Jarl Torg's stunned men were coming to their senses and prepared to close in on her. She expressed a silent plea to Odin just as the battle horn sounded.

For a moment Dalla's arm sank to her side. She raised her sword and looked around, ready for more of Torg's warriors to challenge her.

Jarl Torg's men barely registered what was happening as a small group came from behind the hillside. Men started to pour into the circle, slicing and grunting as the battle rang out.

Dalla dropped Torg's head and sprung into action. Her spirit rose as she slashed through enemy after enemy with Torg's sword. Each fallen man was an unspoken revenge paid for the loss of her jarl, his wife, his daughter and most of all, his son; Bjarke. She cut through the last man for him. She was panting wildly, struggling to catch her breath as she glimpsed at the carnage surrounding her. She felt satisfied. Her sword raised as a man approached her. He was towering, broad, and his sea-foam colored eyes stared at her through his blood-splotched face.

Her heart was pounding as her eyes took him in. She could not believe he was alive. She could not believe the Gods had answered her prayers, and that they had saved him. She released her sword and knelt down before him, her eyes on the ground. She could sense his eyes on her, scorching her. After a long moment she felt his rugged hand take her arm and pull her up from the ground. He hauled her against him for a moment, his chest rising and falling against her as his eyes locked on hers. She could feel the hardness of him pressing against her thigh. She was mortified when a groan escaped her.

Before she pulled away his lips crushed against hers, his mouth tasted her and with each flicker of his tongue against hers she surrendered herself to him as he claimed her mouth. Her hands moved to the back of his neck as she kissed him back. She chastised him with her lips. He could have died.

He drew back and clutched her tightly, wetness pooled between her thighs as her belly tightened. Where was he taking her? Was he still furious with her for what she's told him about his brother, Fleinn?

"Bjar--" She did not get to finish. As soon as they had reached the closest tree just over the hill, he pinned her against it with his hips. His lips captured hers again, making the pain of the bark against her back seem insignificant.

He pulled back only long enough to tear her clothes from her body. She moaned and shivered as the crisp air kissed her naked flesh. His eyes barely looked over her naked body before he was kissing her again. His hand covered her breast. His fingers teased her nipple, tugged at it lightly until it stood at attention for him. His warm skin made her shudder with excitement.

He continued to kiss her, to taste her. Her hips rose to greet his, something primal was taking over within her. She wanted him. She needed to be as close to him as she could. His generous hand drifted further down her body and between her thighs. The low growl in his throat sent hot heat to the very place his finger was caressing.

He freed the leathers of his pants and pushed himself between her legs, his hips pressing forward to grind himself against her opening. She groaned as he gripped the backs of her legs and sank into her, his lips never leaving hers. He devoured her moans as he pushed inside of her. He filled her and left her needing more each time he withdrew from her.

"I want to take my time with you, Dalla, but I cannot. I need you. I need to feel you squeeze around me. I want to hear you cry out my name as I send your mind and body to the stars." His gravelly voice made her insides tremble.

His hands moved behind her neck, as she wrapped her legs tightly around his center, hooking at the ankles behind his back. His fingers locked into her hair as he pulled her face towards his.

"I have lost almost everything. But tonight I have gained you."

Something about his possessiveness made her heart flutter in appreciation. She wrapped her arms around him. Their bodies were flush together from their noses to their thighs. He rocked into her harder, faster and rougher against the tree.

"Gods, I thought you might have died. I thought you were

one of the many bodies on the ground," his throaty whisper swept across her lips.

"I feared the same," she conceded, her voice rivaling his in urgency and desire.

She had never before felt like this. She had never before lain with a man face to face. She had never felt so equal. He grunted louder, and she matched him as she started to climb. To where, she wasn't sure, but she was soaring, the pleasure she felt unlike anything she could have imagined or had ever experienced.

He put his arms under her bottom, holding her against the tree as his hips rocked and thrust. The feeling of him inside of her was almost unbearable as his head lowered so his lips could meet with hers again. She wished his lips would stay there. She loved the taste of his mouth. His grunts gave way to moans of pleasure which pushed into her mouth. The muscles of his body were tightening as his breathing started to increase. It felt as if he were utilizing every muscle to marry their bodies. She could feel the sweat starting to gather between them, allowing their bodies to glide against one another.

"Let go, Dalla. Let go with me." His voice was thick and strained, he slammed himself into her fervently a few more times, and at his request, she let go. Her fingernails sank into the back of his shoulder. Her body shook with his as they both came together. Their voices calling out in synch as they fell.

Bjarke kissed every inch of her shoulder, then her neck as she caught her breath and tried to make sense of what had transpired between them. He remained deep inside her, still hard. His lips found hers again, and he kissed her, tenderly.

Gently. And gradually he released his hold on her and put her feet on the ground.

She stared up at him but did not let him go. She was not sure she was strong enough to stand on her own two feet. What they had just shared had been more primal, more dizzying, just more than anything she had ever experienced before.

He stared down at her, just the same, his eyes unlike she'd known them before. They were not full of mirth or stubbornness. She had seen eyes like his before, enamored, as if he were enchanted by her.

His familiar cocky smile forced her back from her bewitched thoughts. She had never known Bjarke to assert amorous feelings for a woman. She'd never known him to express anything but satisfaction or dissatisfaction. Fear seized in her chest as she realized that he had finally tasted her. There was no longer a reason for him to desire her or chase after her. She swallowed back the disappointment she suffered at the thought. She would not be the woman that Bjarke dismissed. He could handle her rejection, but she would not be able to handle his. She released him and clung to the tree behind her as she lifted her chin and steeled her voice, "You have had your fun and had a taste of the Black Widow, now go."

In an instant, the warmth left his eyes and withered as she'd intended. Bjarke stepped back with a growl and she struggled to keep her hands from reaching out for him.

He tugged on his bottoms, his face steeled with ire. "Do not worry. I have to care for our people until my older brother Sigurd has returned to take his place as jarl." The words traveled through clinched teeth. "Torg's blood was mine to shed. And you stole it from me. I will never forgive you."

CHAPTER 9

Dalla waited for Bjarke's figure to disappear completely before going towards the lake. The blood from battle and the soot from the fires still clung to her skin. She wandered into the water, her body still naked after the tryst with Bjarke against the tree.

Everything they'd built in the village was now gone. They would be starting over with nothing but the clothes on their backs and the weapons in their hands.

The water was cold, so she kept her bathing short. As she moved back to what remained of the village, she happened upon the Seer, standing on the ashes of his home. He approached Dalla as if he'd been waiting for her. The elderly man greeted her when she got close.

"Come, my child, I am in need of your ears." He seized her by the hand and tugged her aside. She was still naked but the Seer could not see. The Gods stole his eyes so that he could hear them.

"What is it?"

He captured both her hands in his and clutched them tightly. The urgency in his grip frightened her, not that she would admit it if anyone were to ask her.

"I see The Bear and his cub followed by a Raven. The Raven will bring nothing but pain and suffering. He must stay away from the Raven and have it killed lest it kill him and those he loves. You must tell The Bear what I have seen. Once things have been set in motion, it will be hard to reverse them."

She mulled over his words for a moment. The only raven she knew of, aside from her older brother who she hoped no longer drew air into his lungs, the only person in the village with black hair, was herself. She blinked back tears at the realization that she was going to bring death upon Bjarke. That she was perhaps the reason for the death of his father, mother and sister, for those were the only ones he loved, aside from his brothers.

"Thank you. I will tell him." With shaking hands she left the Seer and went to find clothes before beginning her pursuit of Bjarke. She reached Catrin's home and found relief that she was inside and safe. Catrin's home had somehow missed the fire and was now filled with children and maidens that had survived the attack.

"Dalla!" Dalla's friend opened her arms and took Dalla into them, hugging her tightly. "I was so afraid that everyone I knew had gone to be with the Gods."

"No, Catrin! Thank the Gods you are alive."

"And you, my friend." Catrin pulled back and searched Dalla's face. "Tell me," Catrin began. For a moment Dalla feared she knew of what had transpired between her and the new jarl in the woods. "… how did it feel to hold a man's head in your hand?"

Dalla swallowed hard, relief washing over her. Her secret was intact. She shook her head at the question only her dearest friend Catrin could utter. "I wish to never hold a dead man's head in my hand again." Dalla's eyes bounced around Catrin's home, in search of what she'd come for. "My home has burned, Catrin, and I am in need of some clothes."

"What happened to yours?" Catrin's wide blue eyes grew larger. "I was not there, Dalla, did he...?"

"No, I burned them," she coolly lied. It was a skill so possessed from her days as an orphan, not one she was particularly proud of but it had suited her well, kept her safe. "After the slaughter I had too much blood and debris upon them. Do you have any extras? I will hunt for you so that you may make more."

Catrin made her way through the crowd flocked around her fire and snagged a spare pair of clothes. She came back and draped them over her friend's chest. "Every woman in the village should be honoring you with a pair of clothing, Dalla. Without you we would not have lived."

Dalla felt the color in her cheeks at the compliment. She did not think of herself as a savior. She was a survivor. The two were very different. "Thank you, Catrin." She dressed hurriedly and then regarded her friend. "I must go. I have a message from the Seer that must be delivered to Bjarke."

"I am sure Bjarke will wish to thank you properly for saving our village." Catrin grinned, and winked, making it clear she was not speaking of verbal gratitude.

Dalla frowned. "Catrin! You must stop this now. His father and mother and sister have just perished."

"Mourning men need some comforting, Dalla. Would you not wish to lie with him?"

She shook her head. "No. I would not wish for that. It would strip away all of my power and status."

Catrin put her hand on Dalla's arm and gave it a squeeze. "Then you must not wait. Bjarke needs his message and you must get to helping to repair what has been lost."

Dalla nodded, silently thanking her friend for understanding, and then she left.

As she searched the homes, and the faces of people working to rebuild their homes, she began to doubt if she should share the message with Bjarke. If he knew he might kill her outright, but perhaps if she stayed away and kept her distance she could save her own life and spare him the pain the Seer had promised. She was about to head towards the woods when her eyes clashed with Sokki's, who had come to a stop in front of her. "Sokki. The village owes their lives to you."

He smirked. "No. They owe it to you, Dalla. I knew he would not fall for my pretty face." Half his face was bandaged. The bandage covered one of his eyes.

"Where are you going?" She glanced around behind him to see if he were being followed. He was alone.

"I need to speak with Bjarke. There is a niggling in my head that he will try to drown me. Will you not grant this warrior a kiss now?" Humor shone in his eyes as his lips quirked up into a teasing smile.

The Bear and his cub followed by a Raven. The Raven will bring nothing but pain and suffering. He must stay away from the Raven and have it killed lest it kill him and those he loves.

As she stared Sokki she realized that he would be the perfect way to keep Bjarke away from her. "Sokki, there is something that I must tell you."

Sokki's grin faltered as he noticed the rush of emotions cross her face. "What is it, Dalla? What has happened?"

She swallowed hard and wedged her hands underneath her arms. "I do wish to tell you. But out here is not the place. Do not keep him waiting, Sokki. Come find me later. I will be staying with Catrin or somewhere nearby."

Sokki hesitated. She could tell that the wait was going to cause him grief. He nodded and departed, leaving Dalla once more alone.

CHAPTER 10

Bjarke turned as he heard footsteps approaching him from behind. He was still on edge from the attack on his people. The devastation of his loss had yet to sink into his heart. He was still burning from his post battle encounter with Dalla. Although she'd spoken those words, it did nothing to control him from wanting her. She was every bit as perfect as he'd imagined, better even. And it would be an eternity, maybe, before he would forget the feel of being inside of her, the sound of her cries of satisfaction as their bodies became one.

Sokki stopped when Bjarke's eyes landed on him. He appeared hesitant and ready to flee. "Bjarke? There is some unhappy news that I must share with you. "

His eyes drifted over Sokki's battered form unhurriedly. He had discovered from other villagers that it had been Sokki's courage that had saved at least half a dozen villagers from their demise. And it was Sokki who had helped Dalla defeat Jarl Torg. His jaw twitched at the hatred he felt for the man whose head was on a pike in the middle of their village.

There would be no Viking funeral for that man. "How long before you can fight with us again, Brother?"

Sokki blinked at him with his one good eye. "Seven moons, maybe more, brother. Are we raiding soon?"

"Yes and I need someone here who I can trust. Someone who our people trust. You are that man."

"Do you trust me, Bjarke? Before the raid you were ready to send me to Hel."

"Before the raid I was going to cut your balls from your body... after punching you in that pretty face a few times." He let the shore fill in the silence for a moment. "You are the only warrior who moved to save my family. You've given blood for me. Not only last moon. I trust you. "

"...Bjarke, we have just received a bird. Your brother Sigurd ran into trouble on his raid."

Bjarke closed his eyes and turned his head away from Sokki. He did not want to hear of more of his family no longer roaming the same soil. "We will wait for his return, Sokki. You may go now, my friend." His gaze shifted back to the water, dismissing him.

Sokki said no more, leaving Bjarke to be alone with his thoughts. Not that he wanted to be alone with his thoughts. All he could think of was Dalla despite his attempts to push his mind towards something more productive. Perhaps if he could concentrate he could think of inspiring words to tell his people. Words that might help them to overcome the injustice and the terror they faced.

Bjarke stood there a little longer and skipped one more stone. He was in no rush to go back to the village and cast his eyes upon the ruins there. But he realized he was now jarl, and the village was depending on him to lead them. As he wandered back towards the center of the village, he allowed himself to process things. It would take months for the village to be as it was. It would not be rebuilt without everyone's hands pitching in. He proceeded towards his neighbors and commenced helping people rebuild and prepare their dead. The moon rose again before he settled down in the small shelter he'd built for himself. He was bruised, tired, and he ached, both from battle and from physical labor.

There was a bowl of stew waiting for him beside the small fire pit on the far side of the small space. It had only been one moon since he'd eaten but it felt more like twenty and his stomach rumbled at the gesture. He sat on the ground and ate the cold soup with vigor and too quickly the bowl was empty. His stomach clenched tightly, it wanted more. He wondered who had given him the stew. Was it Dalla? He would have thought it was Astri trying to win back his good graces, but she and Engli had been among those murdered.

A familiar male laugh outside mixed with a feminine voice pulled him from his thoughts; Sokki. Bjarke grunted as he rose and stepped through the door to see who Sokki had laid his eyes on this time. Sokki had his arm draped around a woman, his lips were by her ear. Sokki appeared drunk and Bjarke wondered where he'd found the mead. The woman to whom the voice belonged was concealed from Bjarke's view by Sokki's substantial body.

Bjarke envisioned Dalla tucked under Sokki's arm and for a moment he felt a fierce jab of resentment in his chest. He started to walk towards Sokki but stayed himself. What Dalla did was not his concern. She was not his concern. His concern was the village, everyone in it, not only Dalla.

Sokki felt a presence behind him and twisted around after

his hand grasped the female's round backside. The female gasped, Bjarke swore the voice belonged to Dalla, but the woman was tucked away in the darkness. "Jarl? Did you wish something of me?" Sokki asked, considering him with his good eye.

Bjarke tried to wipe away the irritation that was distorting his face. He tried to persuade himself that the woman with Sokki was no doubt someone other than Dalla. It was most likely the God Loki playing tricks on him, having a jest at his expense. He cleared his throat and shook his head. "Do not call me that," he said gruffly. "And heal fast Sokki. We raid Torg's land soon. I need a strong arm and quick mind to keep this village safe while we're away."

Bjarke angled away from the two and went back to his hut.

Inside it was slightly chilled, so he stoked the fire. Once the fire was burning, he peered into it for a few moments. The flames of the fire grew and morphed into something bigger, more dangerous. And then he saw flashes of the Great Hall burning. The crying screams of his sister surrounded him. He shielded his ears with his hands but still he could not escape them. His father. His mother. His sister. The slow agony of their death played in his ears. He collapsed to his side as his chest started to heave as he struggled to breathe as the smoke closed in around him. He was living their torment. His eyes closed tightly as he tried to push the vision away. He was trapped. He was going to die.

Thin fingers smoothed over his brow, comforting him. Finally he could breathe again. He inhaled a deep shaking breath and rolled over to his back, his hands spread on his wide chest.

"Shhh." The sound came from sweet feminine lips. He kept

his eyes closed, not wanting to erase the image of Dalla he had in his head even though she was the most ornery of women. He felt his pants loosen, the same warm touch brush over his member, trying to waken it.

"You have come to apologize to your yarl?" he murmured as his cock started to wake and fill out. He felt a soft hand curl around his shaft, stroking it with the expertise of a well trained thrall. When he was completely full he felt himself being surrounded by a hot, wet warmth. He had never felt such a feeling before. It was beyond incredible. When he opened his eyes and looked down his eyes met with a young woman's. He had never laid eyes on her before. He would have remembered her large, bright green eyes rimmed in gold.

Her mouth was stretched around his cock. He had never had a woman's mouth around his cock before. As if she could read his thoughts she smiled around it as her ass moved back and forth in a feline manner.

He pushed away the sex haze. This was not right. This woman was a stranger. Maybe she was a dream. Why would he be dreaming of her? He growled as he pushed her away from his aching shaft. "Stop! Who the hell are you?"

She looked a bit hurt. "I wish to be your bedslave, yarl Bjarke. I will make you very happy. Please let me show you." She moved towards him ever so slightly.

She froze when he shook his head. "I would have taken you to my bed and split you in half... over and over again. But I do not know who you are, woman. Leave."

Her face crumpled as she sat back on her haunches, hands on her thighs. "Please? I have nowhere else to go." A few tears sprung from her green eyes which only seemed to shine brighter. "Being a bedslave is the only trade I have. Please, my Lord, I beg of you." She put her hands together and pressed them to her lips, the tears beginning to run in streams down her face.

"I will not be here much longer to warrant having a bedslave. Seek yourself another warrior to satisfy. Or a farmer for all I care." He pulled his pants on as he stood.

She wiped at her tears, nodded, and looked down at her hands. "I am so sorry, my yarl. I shall go."

"Are you married?"

"No longer. He died. No family to sell me so I fled and threw myself at your mercy, My Lord." She kept her eyes down. "I am seeking a new husband who would split me in half. Over and over." She left without another word.

The Bear shook his head. It would have been a lie if he'd claimed he had not wanted her a little. He shook his head as the visions of Dalla's beautiful face scrunched up in pleasure moved into his mind. Perhaps he should call the woman back to him. Perhaps it would help to relieve his torture. It was nearly morning and only a few minutes passed before he was disturbed again. He looked up as he rolled his head on his neck.

Dalla was standing in his doorway, a steaming bowl in her hands. "I thought you might be hungry, yarl. I know your mother used to--" Dalla, as smart as she was, stopped herself before she angered him further, "I'm sorry for interrupting you, I thought you would be sleeping." She took one step in, enough to set the bowl safely out of the way, and then stepped back again, ready to take her leave.

He stood up and put his hands on his hips, clenching his jaw tightly as his cock jumped at the sight of her. He ignored it. She was done with him and already moving onto the next man.

"Are you healing him the way you let me heal you? Are you healing others in the same way too? Do you spread your legs for any man who tosses you onto the floor, Dalla?"

CHAPTER 11

Dalla's anger flushed on her cheeks as she stared at the man standing across from her. She knew she had no reason to be angry, her plan to keep him away from her was working. But what he was insinuating was insulting.

"If I do it is no concern of yours."

"That is where you are bloody wrong, Dark Raven." He approached her slowly, like a wild cat ready to pounce on its prey. She lifted her chin and stood her ground. She was not scared of Bjarke, The Mad Bear.

"I am not wrong. Do not pretend you were not in here fucking that young girl. Do you forget I have known you for at least fifteen winters? I know you, Bjarke Marsson. I know you are not selective when it comes to that little piece of flesh between your thighs."

He growled as he pulled her roughly, almost violently, against his chest. He stared down into her eyes and she felt her stomach clench and the place between her thighs moisten.

"You know there is nothing small about my cock. You know too that there is nothing stopping me from shoving it deep inside of you right now. Because I am Bjarke, the Mad Bear, the yarl of Asar."

"If you wish to keep it you would be wise not to." She put her hands on his chest and pushed him away roughly. Inside she was quaking, the physical desire for him to do as he threatened was almost unbearable. But he was not for her. She would be the death of him as the Seer prophesied. She had to protect him so that he could live his legacy and father his cubs and lead their people to something better.

He let her push him, his arms falling to his sides for a moment as he stared her down. She watched the muscles in his jaw pop and then disappear. "Stay away from Sokki. I need him to be alive."

"If I do not marry him he will be safe from harm."

"He will not. I will kill him if you go anywhere near him."

She felt the anger burning in her gut. "You cannot tell me who I may and may not lie with!"

He chuckled, though there was no humor in his laugh. His voice was barely contained, "I can. I am your yarl. And you will obey my orders because you have pledged your fealty to me." He slammed his closed fist against his chest for extra emphasis.

She did not frighten easily. And she knew a temper tantrum when she saw one. She closed the distance between them, making slow and deliberate steps towards the man in front of her who was breathing as heavily as if he had just outrun a large army.

"Do you really believe it wise to cross your shieldmaiden?

The one who fights with you and protects your backside with a shield and her own life?"

He spit on the floor at her feet. "You are not my shieldmaiden."

His words struck a chord in her chest and before she registered what she was doing her hand slapped the skin of his cheek. This was it, this was her chance to walk away from him and yet she'd slapped him, taunted him. Surely he would react with force and come at her stronger.

His face remained turned to the side, his cheek turning an angry shade of red in the shape of her hand, which burned like fire.

When his ice blue eyes finally met with hers she felt her pulse hammering in her neck. Her mind was telling her she should run but her body was frozen under his gaze. He stepped forward and grabbed her hair and crushed his lips to hers. She knew it was coming and yet still it shocked her.

She moved backwards, having no choice as he started to move forward as he continued to kiss her like a man starved. Her hands went to his face, her fingers curling in his short beard. This was the last time, she told herself. This was the last time she would lay with the bear.

He released her hair and pushed her to the ground. His smoldering eyes remained on hers as he untied his pants.

The longer she lay there the stronger the urge grew to get up and bolt. He was teasing her because he knew he could.

She sat up but before she could move his hand was in her hair again, tugging her onto her back. "Tell me you do not want this." He growled.

She gasped as his fingers ran along her swollen slit, gathering her juices. He brought his fingers to his mouth and sucked them off. She had never seen anything as arousing as that. She groaned and tried to kiss him but his hand held tightly in her hair.

"Tell me you want your yarl." His offending tongue moved to her exposed neck. She closed her eyes tightly to try to concentrate on the words instead of the ache between her legs that begged for relief.

"Do not tease me, Bjarke." She would not admit to him that she wanted him. She couldn't. He might try and use it against her later when it was convenient for him.

"I am not teasing you." His hand held onto his cock as he pressed the tip to her entrance. "This is teasing you." A moan curled in her throat. as she tried to thrust her hips towards his, he pulled it away.

"Do it or let me go," She said through gritted teeth. her hand wrapped around his and pulled him to her opening.

Both their hands flew away in a flurry as he slid into her. Their mouths were meshed together as she rose to meet each thrust. The first time had not been a fluke, the second was just as mind-melting. There was something between them, at least she felt it.

With each thrust into her she came closer and closer to the edge. She knew now what the edge was, she knew the destination. Her hands moved to his back, clinging to him.

He broke his kiss leaving her lips swollen. "You are mine, Dalla. You will not lie with Sokki."

She dug her nails into his back as she grabbed onto his lower lip with her teeth. "Shut up."

He growled when she drew blood and kissed her again. The passion between them growing hotter and wilder. He grunted louder and pulled back when he finally released his seed deep in her belly with a long, low groan.

She pushed him away when he was finished. He relented but held tight to her knees when she tried to sit up. "I am not finished with you yet, Dalla. You will not want him after I have shown you what I am capable of."

She grabbed onto his head with a frown and tried to pull him away but he was stronger. Between her thighs he crept, his warm tongue raking over her still swollen cunt.

"Ah!" Her hips shot upwards and his head followed as his tongue flickered over her. There was something about that spot that made her want to curl her toes and scream out. He pulled away and looked up at her from between her thighs.

"Do you wish me to stop?"

She grabbed onto his hair and pulled him back down. "Do not st--" She gasped as he hit the same spot while his fingers slammed into her. And he didn't until she was screaming, panting, writhing and coming all over his fingers.

"Do not," he said as he wiped at his mouth and beard with his large hand, "touch another man." He grabbed her knee and pushed it to the side, closing her legs.

She watched as he got up and dressed himself. Her mind was a jumble and there was a sinking feeling in her chest she could not explain.

Before she could try to form words he was gone.

CHAPTER 12

Bjarke moved to the center of the small village. He nodded as he passed by familiar faces. There was one damaged face in particular he was searching for and he was pretty sure he knew where to find it. Without announcing himself he stepped into Sokki's tent, made crudely of sticks and furs. Sokki was sitting on the floor, scratching into a stone and looked up when Bjarke came towards him.

He stood up just as Bjarke grabbed his furs. Through gritted teeth, with anger barely contained, he spoke, "You can have any woman except her. You stay away from her. She is mine."

A flicker of unease and confusion crossed over his face. "Who are you speaking of, Bjarke?"

Bjarke growled as he released Sokki. "You will address me as your jarl!"

Sokki stood up taller, clearly not ready to back down, "My apologies, my jarl. Who is this woman you are commanding me to stay away from?"

Bjarke growled. "The woman you have been making eyes at, grabbing in the daylight, breaking bread with as the moon appears. You know damn well who I am speaking of."

Sokki inhaled deeply. "Dalla? Your shieldmaiden?"

"She is mine."

"You do not wish to marry--"

"Enough!" He clenched his jaw tightly. "Aye, I will not marry her. I will not marry any maiden from this village! But mark my words, Sokki, if you go near Dalla again I will kill you with my bare hands."

Sokki's surprise was evident on his face and it satisfied Bjarke. If he could not have Dalla, then no one else would either. "Bjarke, friend, there is something I must tell you. Dalla—"

"I do not wish to hear it," he interrupted. His friend speaking her name was enough to set his fists aching to grab the nearest weapon. "The Great Hall is in need of repairs. Find yourself there shortly and bring three others with you."

Bjarke left Sokki's tent and made his way towards the Great Hall. He had too much anger. He was going to do something he would regret. Day and night the villagers and warriors and any children strong enough had continued working to repair the building. Today he would once again join them.

Nearly half of the hall had been reconstructed by the time Bjarke made his way into his hut that evening. He went to the middle of his small shelter and laid down with a loud grunt. He was so exhausted he could barely keep his eyes open. He would have punched something in anger had he the strength for the last thing he thought about was Dalla and Sokki. Together.

The feeling of soft warm hands and a hot wet mouth woke him from his slumber. It was dark in his hut and as he tried to open his eyes to see who was with him a soft female moan against his neck sent shivers of pleasure through his body. His hand went to the woman's red hair, pulling her back. The woman's face was familiar. His brain slowly unclouded and he frowned at the woman who had begged him to take her, sexually and otherwise the evening before. The woman who had wept and told him her story of being alone and unmarried. Gerd, was her name.

"What are you doing here?" he demanded, a frown on his forehead.

"I am entertaining the new jarl," she coaxed innocently as her hand drifted down to his cock, which had betrayed him and stood at attention for this woman whom he truly did not desire. He clutched her hair tighter and gave her a little shake.

"I did not ask for this."

"No, you did not. But I am willing to give it. Warriors need release. Especially when they are not fighting. You have aggression, my jarl. You may take it out on me."

He blinked as he studied her face. She was not terrible to look at. Her tits were large enough for his taste. He clenched his jaw tightly as he found himself comparing them to Dalla's. Dalla, who refused to give herself to him. Dalla, who insisted on involving herself with Sokki.

He released her hair and laid back, putting his arms behind his head. He was jarl now and he could have this bed slave any time he wished. But tonight was not that night. His voice vibrated in his throat as he looked down at his quickly deflating erection and shook his head at it. "Gerd. Leave me now. My warrior does not want you."

She looked down between his legs and frowned. "But it wanted me mere moments ago." She was still trying to waken it with her skilled hand but it was no use. She let him go and stood up. "If you change your mind, jarl, you know where to find me."

"I would not hold my breath if I were you."

She studied his face for another few moments, the silence growing between them. Finally she stood and dressed. He watched her leave and then pulled the furs up to his waist as he stared into the fire. For too long his mind stayed fixated on Dalla. He had to get as far away from Dalla as he could. Gerd was right, he did have aggression that needed to come out. Heads needed to roll. It would be best if they belonged to the enemy. He let out a heavy sigh.

Sokki could not give her half of what he could. He grunted when he realized his thoughts had turned once more to that shieldmaiden. He wondered why he cared so much. Perhaps because she seemed to care so little. Dalla was different, had always been since the day he first laid eyes on her at the tender age of thirteen. There was something in her blue eyes that held a deep sadness. She spoke like an offended warrior but in her eyes he could see the pain and hardship. She was like a wild dog who limped badly. She made one want to wrap their arms around her if they could get close enough.

It was for that very reason that she had been able to marry at all. Catrin's parents had taken her in and sold her off when she came of age. Without a proper dowry she wouldn't have been worth much more than a slave.

Her husbands had all died in battle. He recalled each one and how she would mourn for them. She would not eat, she would not braid her hair. He watched her always. And it was not long before she had been tied to another man. History was repeating itself. He should not have been surprised. But he was. He did not wish to see Dalla and Sokki together. In marriage or otherwise. But what did Bjarke have to offer her? Not the thing she seemed to desire amongst all things— marriage. Marriage was a binding of two people, it was hope for a long life together, and of forming a family. He would bare no offspring, thus he did not see the point in marriage, especially to Dalla who deserved the chance to hold babes in her arms.

He had been successful in laying with her thus far. The hunter/prey game they played was invigorating. When either of them grew tired of it they could move on.

And Bjarke had warned off the only other suitor he'd seen sniffing around her. Sokki would not dare betray him. And if he did… that would be the end of him.

CHAPTER 13

The raid on jarl Torg's lands were not far from the village of Asar, but it would still take them a solid three days to travel there and back. Bjarke focused on the impending raid as they sailed closer to the unknown forces waiting for them. If jarl Torg had been wise, he would have left a few warriors behind to safeguard his lands while he was away. If he had done so the warriors of Asar may have a battle to fight though very little chance of defeat.

Other the other hand, jarl Torg could have taken all his warriors with him and left his settlement unarmed in which case this seizure would most likely take little to no effort. The village would either bow down or be slaughtered as jarl Torg had done to his people. He would take no pleasure in it either way. His mood was still soured by Dalla, the loss of his family and the messages he had been receiving about King Harvard's latest antics.

The evening before they left to raid Beckby, Torg's lands, a messenger from Gnupar arrived. The jarl of Gnupar, Jarl Egil, had sent the message to all jarl's that King Harvard was strengthening his army. He was sending scouts to each of his lands and demanding that they supply him with fifty of their best, strongest warriors. If those lands did not comply King Harvard threatened to have their village burned, their maidens raped, and their soils salted.

Bjarke was relieved that he had not yet been sent the summons from the King, but the fact that it was on the horizon was more trouble he was going to have to deal with. It weighed on him. But he was not alone. Jarl Egil formally invited Bjarke and the people of Asar to share in his Summer Solstice. There they would discuss how they would go forth with disarming their brutal King.

But that was not all that weighed on Bjarke's mind. Every time he slept he saw Dalla's face when he'd forbidden her to come along on the raid The pained look was one he would not soon forget. She had been crushed by his rejection. He cared more than he wanted to admit that her feelings had been hurt. But she had disobeyed him and she had deserved the punishment he'd dealt.

Bjarke's ships had arrived midday and without stalling, they were pushed onto the sandy shores of Beckby. Bjarke and his fellow Vikings poured out, with shields already barred they stood in formation against jarl Torg's remaining men which they outnumbered three to one.

A middle aged man with a long graying beard stepped forward, his hand raised as he assessed Bjarke's men. "I am Tulston. Our jarl left me in charge. Who comes here?"

Bjarke stepped forward as well and lowered his shield, "I am Bjarke, Jarl of Asar, your jarl murdered my family, all of them. Including my young sister. He destroyed the lives of many of our women and children. Torg is dead, killed by one of my shieldmaidens, but we do not have to shed blood. You may pledge your fealty to me and live. Our homes were destroyed, all of them, and we are in need of new homes. We wish to take some of your men back with us, in good faith, to help repair our village so that you will not have die here this day."

There was silence as Tulston considered the proposition. "How do we know you will be true to your word?"

Bjarke grinned and shook his head. "You do not know it for certain. I do, however. I give you my word as a warrior of Odin. I live by my honor. I will do as I say. Hurry now, Tulston and make your choice. Featly or death. Which will you choose?"

Bjarke drew his sword and pointed it at Tulston's heart.

Bjarke saw the hesitation on the man's face. Truly if it were reversed Bjarke would not bow. It was not in his blood to be weak or refuse to defend his people. But after a few moments and a sharp pinch of the tip of Bjarke's sword, Tulston dropped to his knee and bowed his head. "I, Tulston, son of Torg, pledge my fealty to you, jarl Bjarke. My sword and shield are yours to use as you please."

"I swear as jarl of Asar that we shall prosper together." Bjarke nodded to him and took a step backwards.

Tulston nodded his approval and his honor as he stood up.

When Bjarke was satisfied that Tulston was not going to provoke them, he turned to the others. "Put your weapons away. We break bread with our new people. We leave before the sun sets to return to Asar and hastily rebuild. We have many plans and they cannot be executed until we have homes for our families to live in while we are away."

The people of the village set their weapons down and once the warriors did the same, they came forward and began shaking hands and exchanging family names. It was the honorable thing to do and built trust amongst the villages. As they exchanged formalities, they were led to their Great Hall, which was intact and much larger than Asar's had been.

Bjarke moved along with them to join the others at the Great Hall, his eyes taking in everything. He did not think they would raise up against him but there were no guarantees. Had they been defeated he doubted his people would have so easily accepted new leadership nor new neighbors into their lands.

He and his warriors sat down, filling many long wooden tables. When the bread was sent around Bjarke noted that it was not also being shared with Tulston's people.

"Why do you not join us in breaking bread? If you word not honorable?" Bjarke was alert, his eyes dashing around the edges of the Great Hall, searching for danger.

Tulston put his hand on Bjarke's forearm and shook his head. "No. Our harvests did not do well. We will not have enough to make it through the winter."

Bjarke pulled his arm away and frowned as he looked around the Great Hall. Is this why Torg had slaughtered his people? It did not justify his actions, but it would explain his motivations. His people were starving. He stood and looked down at Tulston until he had done the same and they stood eye to eye.

"Come, show me your fields. Let me see the state of your farms."

Tulston glanced to his people who were poised at their

tables, watching the two leaders. He looked back to Bjarke. "My jarl, I was wondering if perhaps you knew if my sister was still alive."

Bjarke turned his head to look at Tulston. "I was not aware that any women warriors had come ashore. What does she look like?"

"She is not a warrior, my jarl. She is the jarl's daughter. Gerd knows how to be alluring. She is shoulder height, long red hair, green eyes rimmed in gold." Tulston shook his head. "She insisted on going with our father. I think she was more interested in making sure her lover did not come to harm."

The muscles of his jaw tightened as Tulston named the little minx who had been trying so hard to get into his bed: Gerd. "Yes, she still lives."

He seemed to brighten at the news. "She is?"

"Yes."

"Perhaps, as good faith, to ease the distrust amongst my people, you would take her into your home and marry her?"

"I am here and you have pledged your fealty to me. Why must I marry her? Your sister is a liar."

Tulston frowned. "Perhaps she was lying to make sure she survived. If you had known she was Torg's daughter—"

Bjarke raised his hand, cutting him off. Bjarke thought about the proposition. He had no desire for Gerd but it would be a good move to marry her to prove that he truly had come in peace and that he meant these people no harm. And perhaps more hands would come to help if there were also the promise of a wedding with plenty of food, of which Beckby was in limited supply. This union with Gerd would provide him with what he needed now that he was jarl—a woman to entertain other jarls come to visit while he is gone, a woman to look after the women and children in his absence. Gerd had been raised to do just that. Dalla may have some hold on him but it did not mean he should give up this opportunity to grow their territory peacefully and help these people as well. He would make it clear to Gerd that this was not a marriage of love, but of politics. And because it was a marriage of politics Gerd would be disappointed that no family would come of their union, but it would not make Bjarke feel badly. He could deny Gerd, he did not care for her. As much as he wished to never marry, he was jarl, and this was a decision of peace and war. Gerd would understand. She would have to.

He took a long sip of mead before speaking, the words seemed to stick in his throat. His eyes stared straight ahead at the people as he struggled to get his words out. "Yes, she has already come to me. I will ask her to marry me and pay the price for her dowry to unify our villages into one."

Tultson grinned at the news. "That will be wonderful, jarl Bjarke. Would you like to announce it? Or shall I?"

"Please, allow me. And after we will go look at your fields." As he moved back into the Great Hall and stepped upon the raised platform at the end, he felt as if he were walking to his death. Would it really be so bad to be married? He was determined that it would not be. The marriage was for their people. Not for himself.

Bjarke stood in the middle of the Great Hall and once his hands were raised the crowd's voices dimmed to a soft thrum. "Tultson and I have agreed that what is best for our people is to combine them with blood. I shall marry Gerd, jarl Torg's daughter, and with the union will also come the union of our villages. To grow and prosper together. In order to prosper we are in desperate need of willing and capable hands to rebuild what your former jarl destroyed. Who of your people will come with us? Your help will be paid for in silver." He looked around as they spoke amongst themselves at his announcement. One by one, men and women started to stand. He nodded as he lifted his cup up in praise. "If you wish to come, please gather some things and meet us at the shore. We will depart at dawn."

CHAPTER 14

The sailing back home to Asar was much more cheerful than the sailing away from it had been. Bjarke's people would be more than pleased with his return of an extra thirty men to help rebuild their village. In his mind Bjarke knew he had done the right thing by agreeing to marry Gerd, but the churning in his gut told him something was still wrong. He ignored it the same as he had ignored his short dreams with Dalla. He was to be married, there was nothing further to be done. Perhaps he could convince her to lie with him as his concubine. Until then he would have to make due with only his eyes upon her and the memories of how it felt to be buried deep inside of her.

As the boats were grounded and everyone unloaded, he shook the thoughts from his mind, bringing them back to the present. He glanced across the open land and externally he was smiling as families came to reunite with each other. In his heart he was sad that there was no one to greet him. He wondered how long he would miss his mother, his father, his little sister, his older brothers. He would be glad to see Hedin and Thorvald when they finally returned from their raids.

Bjarke searched the crowd, and when he realized he was searching for Dalla he growled. He commanded his feet to carry him to his makeshift house. As he went he noted that most of the buildings now had their frames completed. It would not be long before the visitors would be returning to their lands to harvest their remaining crops, their arms full of silver. Bjarke had walked the fields with Tulston and had discovered that their soil had not been renewed. Bjarke insisted all farms toss crushed eggshells and seaweed atop the soil. He was certain the crops would see an increase and hopefully it would supply them enough for the winter.

Winter would be time for trading that would need to be done. He stepped into his hut and paused when he saw Gerd inside. A clean set of clothes were settled by the fire which was still working at filling the hut up with heat. She smiled from his pallet when he entered, her dress falling off one shoulder.

His eyes moved over the gentle slope of her shoulder. "You told me you had no family. Your brother, Tulston, asked after you."

A flicker of worry crossed over her pretty face. The more he got to know her, however, the uglier it was becoming. She was a liar, slippery and manipulative. And he had agreed to marry her for the benefit of their people.

"I didn't think I would ever go back there, my jarl. I was left here by my Father. I didn't mean to deceive you. I just knew that if I told you who I was, you would be brutal and have my head removed from my shoulders." Her eyes cast down to the dirt floor.

He grunted, tugging his shirt off and tossing it to the ground as he pulled his weapons from his belt and put them aside as well.

"Do you desire to send me back, my jarl? I will go if that is what you wish. But...I would miss you."

Bjarke scoffed as he started to untie the string of his pants. "He also said that since they swore fealty to me, that they would like me to marry one of their women."

She tried not to look hopeful as she stared at him, her eyes dropping to his pants. "Oh? Did you bring someone home?"

"I did not," he disclosed as he pushed his pants down and moved towards her.

"Did you speak with Tultson then? About a dowry?"

He laid down beside her and put his hands behind his head. "I did. He will receive it after we are married."

She ran her hands up his legs slowly as she moved between them. "Would you like me to demonstrate you care this moon, my jarl? Show you how generous of a wife I will be to you?" She licked her lips which widened with a gasp when he held her away from him.

"No. Our marriage will be one of appearances. I am doing this as a favor to your brother and your people. You will not lie with me except to share my heat to ward off the cold. Is this understood?"

Her eyes flashed with anger but she nodded curtly. "Yes, my jarl, I understand. And what of offspring? An heir to take over after your rule?"

"I am barren. There will be no heir one way or another," he sneered.

"And what of my desires, my jarl?"

"You have a hand, do you not? Use it to keep yourself satisfied."

"And what of your desires, my jarl?"

Again he scoffed. "What I do with my needs is not your concern. Your concern is with being a good wife and looking out for the wellbeing of the women and children in the village. Do that and I will allow you to stay here with us. Refuse and I shall send you back to your village and let you watch as we slaughter them all as jarl Torg unmercifully did to my people."

She gave him a nod before standing up. Her footsteps were silent as she stepped towards the door, "I shall fetch you some nourishment, jarl. I will return shortly."

He watched her go and when she was gone, he laid back with a groan. Alone in his tent with the heat surrounding him, his cock swelled. He moaned as a vision of Dalla popped into his head. He opened his eyes and raised himself to his elbow. He stared down at his dick and shook his head at it. "What do you know? Nothing. Go to sleep." As he stared at it he could imagine Dalla sinking down onto him. He groaned and closed his eyes again.

He pulled his pants on roughly before standing. There was no way he was going to be getting any sleep, not without spilling his own seed upon his belly first. And that was not something he wanted to do. He pulled his shirt on and stepped outside into the fresh air. He inhaled deeply as he made his way through to the village to see how the visitors were getting along with his people. Everyone seemed to be working, save for the Seer. But it was not his job to work.

As Bjarke drew closer, the Seer smiled wider. "Jarl. I have been expecting you. Did Dalla pass the vision on to you?"

Bjarke frowned at his words. Dalla? What did she have to do with anything? "I do not recall her saying anything."

The Seer nodded. "I did not think so. I had a vision, jarl. Would you like to hear it?"

Bjarke frowned, glancing around. "Yes, Seer, of course. Your visions are always true, wise and a gift from the Gods." Bjarke gently drew the Seer aside and once they were away from spying ears, he stopped them. "Please, now share the vision."

"The Bear and his cub are followed by a Raven. The Raven will bring nothing but pain and suffering. He must stay away from the Raven and have it killed lest it kill him and those he loves."

Bjarke took the words and repeated them in his head a couple of times. Followed by a raven? Bjarke looked up at the sky, the white clouds were sailing against the brightest blue. It was indeed a beautiful day. No birds of land overhead, just sea gulls. "Can you tell me more?" he asked, "I do not know what the vision is trying to make me see."

"Beware of the Raven," he repeated, "Beware of the blackened hair."

"There is only one I know who dons blackened hair. You gave the vision to her."

The Seer shook his head, "I cannot say more than this. I did not see more than this, Jarl Bjarke."

As the Seer stumbled away, Bjarke's mind was already cloudy with the only black haired person he knew. His jaw clenched tightly as the words ran through his mind. It was no wonder Dalla did not share with him the Seer's vision. She clearly did not wish to die. He frowned at the thought of having to kill her. And what did the Seer mean by a cub? He was barren. The vision made no sense. Perhaps he had it wrong. With purpose and clenched fists at his side, Bjarke headed towards the edge of the village. He would seek her out.

He did not make it past the town's center before he stopped himself. The Seer had just warned him to stay away from the Raven and here he was moving towards it. He growled and turned around yet again. He had better things to do than to step right into his own death. His cock wanted nothing but Dalla but it did not rule him. His people needed him now, to marry Gerd, to be an honorable, strong jarl. With a newly steeled resolve that was exactly what he intended to do. He would not disgrace the good name his father had given him. It was for his family that he made his way towards the Great Hall to help with the repairs.

CHAPTER 15

SUMMER

Dalla heard in the distance the cheers of the village raise as she assumed Bjarke and his new bride were exchanging their wedding kiss. She couldn't stomach watching it. If it hadn't been for the Seer and his words, she might be the one kissing Bjarke. She'd managed to avoid being present at the ceremony but she knew she would be missed at the Great Hall for the post-ceremony celebration and that she must show her face there. She wished she wouldn't be missed. She wished she could go back in time before she'd ever listened to the Seer. She wished he'd never shared the vision with her. She closed her eyes and paused beside a longhouse. She pressed her forehead against the freshly sliced timber to let the wave of nausea pass. She hoped she wasn't becoming ill, the feeling of being sick was becoming bothersome.

It was the third time today she'd felt as if she may lose her guts to the ground. She stood up and exhaled slowly before leisurely heading towards the Great Hall which had been completed a few moons ago. It was the completion of this project which had marked the time for Bjarke and his new wife to become married.

Stepping into the Great Hall, she squeezed sideways to move between two large groups of warriors. She winced as her breasts grazed against one of them. She must have been in need of something that only a man could cure, there was no other way to explain why she was so sensitive. She had never had such feelings before. Perhaps it was because she'd never know the feelings she'd felt before. She had vivid dreams of Bjarke every evening. When she woke she was quivering with post-orgasm chills.

When she was past the fire her eyes immediately fell on Bjarke. He was sitting on his high chair next to his beautiful young flaming-haired bride. Their new bands of silver sparkled in the torchlight with each raise of their cups.

She sat down at an empty seat and felt the familiar roll in her belly as a large platter of roasted pork passed by her, on its way to the head table. No, not now, she thought. She placed her hand to her mouth and quickly tried to make her way towards the door. Before she could make it there, her guts heaved. She let it go onto Sokki, who happened to be standing there.

"Dalla!" He had his hands up, her vomit sluggishly rolling down the side of his leg. He put his hand around her back and led them both outside the Hall. "Are you ill?"

Dalla shook her head as she studied Sokki's soiled leg. "I do not think so. Come to my hut and I will wash it for you."

Sokki placed a gentle hand on her shoulder and squeezed until she was looking him in the eyes. "Do not worry. I hope you are well enough to fight. I hear Bjarke is ready to leave on a raid again before the frost comes."

Dalla nodded and watched as Sokki limped away. She sighed. She wished she could feel for Sokki even a tiny bit of what she felt for Bjarke. Bjarke. Married. She still could not believe it. Bjarke had not sought her out upon his return and Dalla could only assume it was because he was engaged to be married. Dalla had observed the two of them carefully over the past couple of full moons. She could see nothing amiss. It seemed Bjarke had finally found someone to love. Gerd was pretty enough and gracious enough. Her skin did not wear the wounds of battle as Dalla's did.

She hated that she was constantly comparing herself to Gerd. She no longer wished to care that Bjarke had given his heart to another.

She clenched her fists hard at her sides and spun on her heel. She was going to eat something in front of Bjarke and not give him the satisfaction of knowing that she wished it were her at his side. Not that she thought he may have guessed it. She had kept her distance from him and he had pretended she did not exist. She searched until she found Catrin and went to sit beside her for the feast.

"Catrin. Did you see the ceremony?"

Catrin grinned at Dalla, partly because she was happy to see her, partly because she loved to speak of others. "It was beautiful. You did not witness it?"

"No. I was at the lake."

"Ah," Catrin cooed and nodded her head knowingly.

Dalla frowned and shook her head. "No, it was not that. I am due to bleed but not for..." she paused and scrunched her brows together as she tried to remember the last time she bled. Oh Gods! She had not bled since before the last raid.

Catrin regarded her with a frown. "Are you alright? Are you ill?"

Dalla put a hand to her tummy. "Yes, I am... I am ill." She rose up gently and put her hand on Catrin's shoulder, squeezing it lightly. "Please tell the jarl I am so happy for him, if you speak with him."

Catrin nodded, though she appeared confused. Dalla had to get away from the Great Hall as quickly as possible before it started to fall down around her. She couldn't be pregnant with Bjarke's baby. She couldn't be! She couldn't have children. Neither could he! And he was married! Married! Five steps before the exit Bjarke's voice boomed towards her as it bounced off the walls of the Great Hall.

"My friends! Brothers and Sisters. I know you wish it, and I shall proclaim it tonight. Soon we raid. Soon we will gain more riches for ourselves to prepare for winter. The trading with our friends to the North on the next moon will stock our homes with plenty to keep us warm and fed." Everyone in the hall was watching him as he spoke. He looked so powerful up there. Gerd reached her hand out and placed it on his arm as she rose with him. The smile on her face showed affection for Bjarke. For a moment again Dalla wished it was her settled there next to him.

The cheers surrounding her now were deafening and Dalla felt as if she were in her own version of Hel. She wouldn't be able to go on the raid. Not now. Gradually she turned around and felt her chest tightening. Time seemed to be playing tricks on her as she watched Bjarke dip his head to Gerd's.

His lips touched her smiling lips. His fingers caressed her cheek.

Dalla's eyes closed as time caught up with her. She spun around and forced her way out into the fresh summer air.

As she walked to her hut, she brought her hand to her stomach, the Seer's vision played through her mind. Perhaps the babe in her belly was the Raven. Perhaps it would have dark black hair like her own. Perhaps this is what would cause Bjarke pain and suffering and death. Tears pricked at her eyes as she entered the darkness of her home. She would have no choice but to lie. She would have no choice but to quickly find a man to lie with, to take claim to her babe, Bjarke's babe, when it came to life.

CHAPTER 16

Bjarke stumbled into his home, his arm around Gerd's shoulders as she helped him to his pallet. The sounds of the village had started to blur a few cups ago. The fire to his right was blurred as was the rest of the pitiful furnishings in his modest longhouse. He fell onto his furs with laughter as the thought of the blessings the Gods had lain at his feet. Crops that were plentiful and would grow, and strong warriors to take the things they needed from others.

Gerd's voice cut through his thoughts, "It does not please me when you are drunk, Bjarke."

The words caused his haze filled eyes to look at her. She was beautiful to look at this night. Her breasts were very ample and more than a handful. Her hips were wide and good for birthing. Why, though, could he not find that fire for her? Why did the fire not stir inside when he gazed at her body? Or any other maiden's body for that matter? He knew. He knew it was because of the raven-haired woman who would be the death of him. He had done a fine job of staying away from her. The Gods should be proud.

"What was that, wife?" he asked her. Their engagement had been less than pleasant. They put on a show for the village but when they were alone, the sparks flew. Unfortunately for his little warrior they were not the sexual kind.

"I said I do not like it when you are drunk. It is unpleasant when I am around you. The mead leaks from your skin and fills the air I breathe. It is wretched."

Bjarke frowned as a fire started to build within him. Not the fire that had burned inside when he fought with Dalla. This fire was anger that wanted to fuel his actions. Actions full of violence.

"The last time I checked, wife... I am jarl, and not you. You are my wife in title, and nothing more. That is your option and the only one. Accept it or you can go back to your brother. I shall drink as often as I please and in whatever quantity I want and you will say nothing to me about it. Do you understand?"

She glared at him, her arms crossed under her chest. "I understand. I understand that I have married my father who was also a no-good drunkard."

He growled as he sat up, pointing a heavy finger at her. "Do not ever compare me to that old butcher, ever again."

"And why not? You are both the same!"

Bjarke came up from the ground and careened into the table before his hands found their target on her shoulders. His grip was tight and he realized it would leave marks upon her perfect skin. "I do not slaughter innocent children. I will never butcher a child as he did. You are lucky that I don't punish you for those words." She winced as he shook her some. "My little sister...." his voice almost broke. As his hands released her he fell back, letting himself fall onto his pallet. He heard the shuffle of her feet as she moved towards the door.

"Leave me and do not say another word. I am tired," he groaned as he laid down onto his side. His head was spinning.

What he didn't say to her that he wished he could have was that he was sorry. So very sorry that she was stuck with the likes of him. It was not her fault that she was Tultson's sister, Torg's daughter. It was not her fault that he did not desire her. He would never be a good husband to her. Not in the way a woman needed.

As the room spun around him through closed eyes, he felt sick. Sick and angry. This was no way for a jarl to act, he realized it. But what was a man to do when he was denying himself the one thing he constantly obsessed over? Finally sleep took him.

Dalla was smiling in the sunlight by the sea. She was carrying a babe. A raven-haired babe that stared up at her in adoration. And she was looking at Bjarke, her hand reached out to him and he reached out in return. He took a step forward and then two, getting closer and closer to her. His heart was pounding and tightening in his chest. His heart feeling like it would beat out of his chest the moment their fingers would kiss.

As he stepped towards her she was stepping away, further and further, holding her hand out to another. His hand kissed with another's. His hopes were dashed the instant Sokki came forward to claim his family and Gerd wrapped her arm around his to claim hers. In her other arm was a sleeping babe with inky black hair.

"We will love them both the same." She said.

He frowned at her and looked down in his arms. There in his grasp was a skeleton. The bones of a babe wrapped in a fur. He wanted to drop it but instead he clung to it though he did not know why. When he looked out to the sea, he saw dark storm clouds. The Gods were angry. Lightning lit up the seas. He looked back down to Gerd's arms but the babe had instead turned to a raven. It cawed loudly in Bjarke's direction before taking flight. He watched in fascination as it dove and swooped. It made a large circle over the woods before coming back to land on Dalla's shoulder.

When she looked back to him he saw the tears on her cheeks, the babe she had been holding was no longer in her arms.

He moved to go to her but Gerd held him back. "She is but a shieldmaiden. She is nothing more than a traitor and a whore. A traitor and a whore." Gerd continued to say the words over and over again. His stomach grew tight. He pulled his axe from its place in the dirt at his feet and raised it overhead. "A traitor and a whore. A traitor and a whore." He grunted with the effort as he brought the axe down upon her head.

Bjarke cried out as he woke from his dream. Sweat had poured from him, the furs beneath him and his clothes were soaked. Gerd was asleep beside him, her head still intact. He rubbed his hand over his face and stumbled outside where he threw up as the image of Gerd with his axe in her head remained.

He wiped at his mouth and went down to the sea. The waves

lapped gently at the shore as he rested upon the rocks. He prayed to the Gods for a sign of what he should do next. Should he promise his men to the defeat of King Harvard in his home of Trelleborg? Or go sailing across the ocean to see what riches he could gather for his village to provide for them as he promised his people? As he stared at the sea, he felt his eyes drifting closed. The Gods were telling him to sleep.

He washed his face in the water and then returned to Gerd. She wasn't there, but she had taken the furs with her so he could only assume she was going to wash them, as a good wife would do. But not his wife. His wife should have servants. He settled down in the middle of the floor and put his arm over his eyes. He would work on getting her servants after he had a little nap, it was least he could do for being such a poor husband, and he hoped in time they would learn to be civil with each other.

CHAPTER 17

The celebration of the union of the jarl and his new wife was only halfway complete. Bjarke had already grown tired of the clinking of metal cups which spurned his demands to kiss his new wife.

He tried to see the good things that came with his union. One of which was the presence of the skalds, singers and poets who were continuously sharing their stories, sagas and songs. The other was the vast amount of food his people and were able to consume. The scents of feast days were incomparable. The freshly baked breads dripping with freshly churned butter, the cheeses and desserts. After three days of feasting the whole community would be full of belly, full of heart. That was what they needed, he reminded himself. That was why he had decided to marry.

The skald was in the midst of the saga of Thor and Thrym when a group of men approached Bjarke's table. It took him a moment to draw his attention away from the entertainment. When he settled his eyes upon the men he immediately sat up straighter.

Gerd sipped at her mead and raised her eyebrow. "Do you know these men, my Jarl?"

"Aye. The jarls of Harvard's lands."

"Aye, and we missed you at the Summer Solstice and regret we are late for your union, Jarl Bjarke. We did not receive ample notice." The oldest, grayest of hair, and most portly spoke. He was wearing the runes of Fjall.

Bjarke cleared his throat. "My apologies, Jarl Unwin. I was not certain when the Great Hall would be completed. It came a bit earlier than we expected."

Jarl Unwin grinned as he regarded Gerd. "It is no surprise, Jarl Bjarke, that you did not wait when you have as beautiful a bride as yours." He bowed his head and Gerd raised her cup to him.

Bjarke stood up and greeted each of them, hand on the forearm to show they were unarmed. "Please, enjoy the feast."

"We plan to partake, Yarl, however, there is some business we need to discuss." Red of hair, white of beard, Yarl Egil of Gnupar, nodded to Gerd.

"Ah, yes." Bjarke glanced at his wife and gave her a nod. "We shall return shortly." He was about to step away when Egil laughed.

"Please do not be modest on our counts." Egil grabbed a fork and tapped it against Bjarke's cup.

Bjarke forced a smile and bent down, placing yet another kiss on Gerd's lips. When he stood he quickly led the men away from the Great Hall and into the adjoining longhouse which would soon be his home. He motioned for them to join him near the fire.

"We apologize for bringing this to your wedding, but it is not something we can wait to discuss."

Bjarke sipped at his mead. "This is about our King?"

"Aye," this response came from a man wearing Hraun's runes. But he was not the same man that Bjarke knew as Jarl Kveldulf. The jarl of Hraun would come each spring to do trade with his father.

Bjarke's gaze narrowed and the man, slightly older than Bjarke with similar blonde hair, long down his shoulders, stood up taller.

"You are not Jarl Kveldulf. I remember him being older than you are now."

He nodded. "Aye. I am Kol. His son. My father is not well and soon it will be my place on his chair."

Bjarke nodded and took another sip of mead. "I hope the Gods take him soon. He will be happy in Valhalla. He can say hello to my father, mother, sister, and brothers." He raised his cup to honor them all. "Back to business at hand so that we may feast. What have I to do with the King? He has not bothered to come here. We are the southmost land for him. We do not bother him. He does not bother us."

Egil spoke up. "This is true, Bjarke, but if we do not go together to defeat him, we will fail and one by one we will fall. Harvard is ruthless and if we go without you and we lose, he will come for your people as well."

"Do not lose." Bjarke said in reply. He was not eager to send any of his men to fight the King.

Unwin crossed his arms over his chest. "He has taken my daughters and my wife, Bjarke. He has taken all six of them. My youngest is but five winters old, was that not the age of your sister?"

Bjarke's jaw clenched tightly at the mention of his deceased sister. "She was seven."

"Can you imagine if the King had come for her? Can you imagine what he would do to her? He is voracious with women. And when they cry too much, he kills them. I have seen it with my own eyes. I do not want—" Unwin's clenched fist came to his mouth as his throat closed off his words.

Bjarke had no choice but to imagine it. It made his stomach turn to think of it. "Why did you not fight?" he asked.

"He came under the cover of darkness," Kol spoke up. "He took them all. When we went to reason with the King, he sent his warriors out to kill us. We have come to warn you that you should have a guard around your wife. He will come for her too and any daughters you birth. He is not healthy in his head and he must be stopped."

"And which of you will step up to take his place? Or are there others you are hoping to recruit?"

The men looked around at each other and shook their heads.

"Perhaps it is best we have no king at all," Unwin said. "We are doing well managing our own people. And the people of Asar are no different. They are prospering and appear happy. We are here on the bequest of our families and those who have put their trust in our leadership. We do hope you will decide to stand with us. We will rise against our King just after Jul, Bjarke. We hope that you will rise with us. Consider it."

Jul was many months away. The hillsides would be covered with snow, the ocean would be iced over and there would be no way for attacks from the sea. He would consider it. He felt in his chest that he already knew how he would decide and he was not looking forward to losing more good warriors to Valhalla.

CHAPTER 18

Dalla had spent all day on the rocks by the sea, begging the Gods to guide her, but they did not seem to want to speak with her. Resigned to hiding from Bjarke, Dalla carefully plucked herself from the shoreline and began her rocky trek back to land. She was almost there when her foot slipped. Her ankle twisted and pain radiated through her foot. She groaned and sank down to steady herself.

"Are you hurt?"

Dalla glanced up to find the source of the unfamiliar male voice. The man was tall, broad of shoulder, light of hair much like Bjarke. He was wearing unfamiliar runes, and it caused her a little alarm.

He held up his hands. "I'm visiting for the wedding feast. I am Kol of Hraun. I have just left your jarl and his new wife feasting in the Great Hall. I do not wish you harm, maiden."

She wished she could believe him, but he was a man. "Why are you out here then? Why are you not feasting?"

He did not move closer and he paused, his lips mysteriously closed.

"You take too long to respond, Kol of Hraun. Go back to the feast and leave me be."

He appeared slightly surprised by her command. His lips curled ever so slightly into a grin. "My dear maiden, I will return as soon as I know you are well. I only wish to help you."

She snorted. "Because I am a maiden I am in need of help?"

Kol's grin grew wider. "No, the twist in your ankle will make it difficult to climb the rocks."

She stood up slowly and stared at him as she took a step forward. "See, I do not require—" She set her foot down and put weight on her ankle. A jolt of pain ripped through her leg, taking her down to her knee.

This man, Kol, was beside her, his arm around her waistline, his other behind her knees. "Help? You do, maiden." He hoisted her up into his arms and swiftly took her to shore. As she started to twist in his hold he set her down. "Do be gentle on your ankle. The more you fight being still, the longer it will take to heal." His eyes roamed her body quickly. "But it seems you know much about healing."

She felt her cheeks color at the mention of her many scars. "That I do." Without another word she swung around and began to hobble back to her home, which had yet to be rebuilt. It was still just a small hut. She had been too busy helping the other women with children to rebuild their abodes first.

"Will I see you at the feast after the moon has come out?"

"No," she replied.

"Because you will be resting?" he asked. His voice was fading away, she could assume he was standing where she'd last seen him.

Dalla had no idea why the man was interested in entertaining her. She glanced back and his grin was still firmly planted on his handsome bearded face. She shifted back around and answered him. "No."

Catrin came down the walkway and paused when she saw the man standing near the shore. Dalla was still hobbling, annoyed that her friend was so easily distracted by handsome male faces.

Catrin's eyes finally noticed Dalla, and she sprung into action, coming close and wrapping her arm around her friend's waist. "What has happened to you? Did that man harm you?"

"I harmed myself. Do you know him?"

"I have heard he is Jarl Kveldulf's son. I heard he was handsome and that he looked much like Bjarke. There is some resemblance there."

Dalla stopped, her heart beating in her chest as she turned and peered at Kol who was still standing in the distance. He did look very similar to Bjarke. And he would soon be returning to his village. And he would have no reason to come back to Asar to claim his babe. Dalla swallowed the lump that had formed in her throat. The Gods had answered her. They'd given her Kol.

"Why are you staring at him, Dalla?"

She looked at Catrin, her best friend, and for once in her life she could not bear to lie. "I have something to confess. And after I do, I will need a favor. A favor that I will repay in whatever way I can. Let us go to my home and I will tell you all of it."

CHAPTER 19

The spray of the water hit his face as he stared at the choppy waters ahead. The sound of the birds calling deafened him as they sailed upon the breeze. His hand held strong to the rope as the boat rocked under foot. Storms gathered behind them, but he was focused on the land growing larger in front of them. This felt right. The boats cut through the water as the warriors gathered their weapons and shields. Everyone prepared. Then with eyes of a bird it seems Bjarke would soar above the boats as they headed towards the land. Those keen eyes showed him farms and people, then a large settlement that seemed lush with gold.

His eyes opened under his large arm which he pulled away. He had been shown his course, and it was still the same. A raid. Bjarke sat up from the hard floor with a groan, the muscles of his back and legs sore.

He grabbed a cup of mead from the table and half of it was consumed before the sleep was out of his eyes. He put the cup down and moved towards the flap of his home and moved out into the sun. The light stung his tired eyes.

Gerd was approaching him, a large armful of furs being stirred in the gentle breeze that blew by as he tried to rub the sleep from his eyes. "Good afternoon, Husband."

"Good morning, Wife." He stepped forward and grabbed the furs from her arms. "You should not be doing these tasks. They are not for a jarl's wife. Decide who you prefer to aid you and I will make it so." He heard her behind him as he made his way back into the longhouse. "And..." He let them fall onto the pallet before turning to her. "We should be making quarters in the Great Hall. That is where the jarl and his family ought to be. And since this evening is the last day of our wedding feast, I will make sure it is done."

She nodded, clearly still angry at him for their evening spat. "I do hope there will be no more ringing cups. I am sure you wish the same."

His jaw ticked with frustration. It was true he did not enjoy the tinkling of metal but he hadn't expected her to notice it. In the end it did not much matter, they were not a love match sent from the Gods. "I will be leaving to raid as soon as supplies and ships are ready. I will leave two ships and four warriors behind for your protection."

"Bjarke, you do not need to leave anyone behind to protect me. You have claimed one large settlement already. Anyone coming here will not gain respect by attacking while you are away. They would gain nothing but the land because we would not lie at their feet and serve them."

He had an ache in his jaw as he held back his thoughts which bordered on dark and evil things, namely a King who apparently had an affinity for other men's wives and little girls. He cleared his throat and bowed to her request. "Then I shall take them all with me. For we will find many treasures to keep our coffers full." He smiled down at her. "Go and find yourself suitable handmaidens and have them help you move our things. I must go make sure the boats are ready and that our guests found much rest, for tonight will be the most jovial evening yet."

He had gone around to three of his guests, confirming that they had a pleasant night's rest. The last for him to speak with was Kol. As Bjarke rounded the corner he spotted Dalla coming from Kol's tent. He felt the fire in his veins going straight to his head. She looked rather happy, her hair was mussed. Had she and Kol just lain together?

She paused for a moment and turned back. Kol appeared in the doorway of his tent and called her back. She smiled and calmly limped to him. He brought his arms around her and she pressed her lips firmly to his.

The muscles of Bjarke's jaw tightened as did his hands at his side.

She nudged him back inside the door and began her limping walk once again. The closer she grew to Bjarke the more her smile faded away until she was standing before him in a near scowl. "Jarl, he needs a moment to clean up."

Bjarke's displeasure was easy to see. So they had lain together. Red started to color parts of his cheeks as his blood started to flow with fire.

She crossed her arms over her chest and smirked as if they were old friends, having a chat after a moon apart. "I did not congratulate you yet. You must be pleased that the Gods have blessed you with such a lovely wife."

Bjarke's eyes burned into hers. He wished to take her into that tent with Kol and ravage her in front of him. He wanted to make her scream and cry his name. He was furious not only that she had lain with another but that he cared so deeply that she had. "Shut up. I don't need your false words," the fury filtered through the words she heard from him.

She frowned, confusion on her puckered brow. "My words are not false. I am happy you have found someone to share your life with. She will make you a wonderful wife and bless you with beautiful children. Is that not what you want?" Her bright gray eyes searched his, what she was searching for exactly, Bjarke did not know. Nor did he care.

Bjarke said nothing to her. The words he preferred to say he would not let out. He was too angry. The frown overtook her face as she moved past him as she limped towards her home. Bjarke turned and watched her and then followed her.

She moved into her hut through the flap and Bjarke stepped in right behind her. She swung around, ready to fight him, her hands curled at her sides. She was so beautiful in that moment and the admission only angered him more.

"How do you know Kol of Hraun? Have you just met him?"

Dalla stared at him, studying him before she lifted her nose into the air. "We have crossed paths before."

"Where?"

"Harvest Feast."

He narrowed his eyes. "How did I not know?"

"You were busy with mead and women."

He was not sure that he believed her. "Why did he not mention to me that he knew you, shieldmaiden?"

"Perhaps it is because he is ashamed. He is the jarl's son. You know the predicament well, do you not?"

He frowned, ignoring her stab at him. "It matters not. I do hope you had a pleasant goodbye. I had a vision. We will leave for the raid when the sun rises and you will come with me." It sounded more like a command then a request, just as he'd intended.

Her brow scrunched up tighter, "I will not."

For a moment surprise appeared on his face. That must have been why she smiled a little. He wished to wipe the smile from her defiant lips. "You will raid or you will be banished from my lands."

She laughed, and he felt his gut tighten further. "You wish to banish me? Fine. I am sure that I could find a place in Torde. It will be easier that way." She turned her back on him as she moved towards the far wall where her trunk was. With a crouch she stood beside the trunk and flipped the lid open violently to begin packing her things.

Bjarke stepped up behind her, his powerful hands taking hold of her shoulders to get her to her feet and spin her around towards him. "Don't you ever turn away from me while I'm speaking to you." He barely closed his eyes in time as her spit covered his face.

"I will do as I please and that angers you. Unhand me!"

His hand rose and wiped her spit from his face. Some of it still clung in his beard. His hand went into her hair and pulled her head back, his other hand sliding to her backside, pressing his hips roughly against hers. Instantly his cock swelled against his pants, he could barely contain himself or the passion he felt for her. "You will do as I please. I am jarl." His words seethed with resentment as he pulled her head forward and his lips pressed forcefully against hers. His body craved hers, his blood leaving his brain so other primal parts could take over.

He felt her shiver against him as her hands came towards his chest. At first they pushed against him, then he felt her fingers curl into his clothing. He so was lost in the kiss, so lost in the desire to possess her that he did not expect her hands to change course again and push him away. He grunted as he was forced to take a step back.

"Is your wife not enough for you, jarl? Is that why you want to bring me raiding with you? So that you may pillage me whenever the mood strikes you? I am not your bed slave. I will never be your bed slave." There was outrage on her face, fury he did not understand nor wish to.

He clenched his jaw tightly. There was so much he wished to say to her. And yet... "Keep packing your things, Dalla. We raid soon." He took a step back and then another but her next words crushed him.

"I cannot go with you. I am with child."

Bjarke was mid-turn when those words drifted through his ears. He should not have come after her. He should have left well enough alone so that he could still see Dalla as a woman with honor and respect. Now he would be tormented with thoughts of her and another man. His dream came rushing back, Dalla with a babe. The Gods had shown him. He had disobeyed them and now he was being punished.

CHAPTER 20

Dalla had stayed in her bed most of the day as the healer had instructed. As she headed towards the rowdy celebration in the Great Hall, the last day of the marriage feast she glanced down at her wrapped ankle. One plate of food and one drink were the instructions from the healer. Then she was to return home. She was not but a few feet away when Kol came outdoors. He glanced around and headed for Dalla upon spotting her. He smiled, and she tried to manage one.

"The evening is just beginning. Why do you not smile?" he asked.

"You are leaving."

His smile flickered, and he shrugged. "Yes."

"I will miss playing Hnefatafl with you. You were a worthy opponent. And it was, as you promised, a wonderful distraction from the annoyance of my ankle."

He smiled. "It was enjoyable for me as well. Perhaps the most enjoyable evening I have spent with a woman."

"That does not speak to your manly charms, Kol." She grinned. It faded as his eyebrows raised and his hand went to the back of his neck.

"Dalla, about the kiss…"

She shook her head with a smile. "I apologize. There is a man in the village that is very persistent. I admit I planted the kiss for my own selfish purposes. Do you forgive me?"

He frowned at her words. "That can be very serious, Dalla. My mother once--"

Dalla smiled sadly and nodded. "Yes. I know. But he is not a threat in that way. I do know danger from stubbornness. I do believe that he will no longer pursue me thinking that I have lain with another."

He studied her face and sighed. "And that is not what you wish."

She frowned, her eyebrows dropping over her eyes. "Certainly it is."

He smiled. "Dalla. I am not sure how many others you have fooled, but I am not one. If you cannot stand to be near him, knowing he has made eyes at another you are always welcome in Torde. Ask for me directly and I will see to it you have what you need."

"That is very kind," she said softly, bowing her head. "Were you on your way?"

"Aye. The travel back to Torde is a long way. I have to prepare for raids."

She nodded and held out her arms. He stepped into her embrace and hugged her.

"Until we meet again, Dalla."

"May the Gods keep you safe."

He nodded. "And you." She watched him walk away until he was but a speck in the distance.

She entered the noisy warm hall and found herself a seat. Bjarke was sitting upon his high chair next to Gerd. She looked like a Queen and Bjarke, a great leader. Catrin sat down next to Dalla and stared up at their jarl. "Are you going to tell him, Dalla?"

She tore her eyes from Bjarke and peered at Catrin. She shook her head and glanced away from her friend's eyes which were full of pity for her.

"Please do not look at me as if I were an old woman with no home."

"How will you care for a child, Dalla?"

"How does any other woman in the village care for a child?"

"With trades. You are not a trades smith. You are a warrior."

Catrin was right, of course. She was a warrior. It was all she knew. And yet she would have to figure something out because the babe was going to come before the next Midsummer solstice.

"I have time to learn a trade. And I would like to think my friend would help me if I were to fall into the mud."

Catrin hugged Dalla gently. "You know I would." Catrin's eyes shifted to the jarl and she let a small chuckle leave her belly. "He looks as if he would rather be tied in a net above a pit of venous snakes."

Dalla noticed and started to laugh. And that was the beginning of her wedding feast. She laughed, sang and was entertained by the skald. Instead of one cup of mead she'd had two and when Catrin made her leave, Dalla did the same, wincing as her ankle took some weight.

She limped through the throng of people until she was finally outside. She inhaled the chilly night air deeply and put a hand to her stomach. She was already starting to show a little. It would be not much time at all before everyone would know.

The babe sapped her energy, more so than any battle she had ever fought. She folded her arms over her chest and limped back towards her home, Catrin leaving her soon after their walk for she lived close to the town's center. Sitting, eating and laughing, as mild as that had been, was still exhausting, and she found herself wishing for sleep. In her dreams she could be with Bjarke, at least, and she longed to be next to him again. Only her fear of harming him stopped her. That and the babe inside of her.

She was almost to her home when she heard her name. She turned around, her eyes falling on Bjarke who was staggering towards her, a cup of mead still in his hand. "Poor Dalla. Where is your Kol now? Oh yes, on his way home."

She turned her back on him and continued to limp, she was nearly there. "Go away. Can you not see I am heart broken?"

He laughed a little too long. "No. I cannot."

She stopped and turned towards him once more. "What do you want?"

Bjarke kept looking at her as he took another drink from the cup. "I came to talk. Came to speak my mind, Dalla," he said as he staggered towards her hut.

"You have already spoken your mind. We have nothing more to say to each other. Go back to your wife and your people. They will miss you if you are gone."

Bjarke stepped through the flap of her hut. He wasn't listening to her apparently, or perhaps he was too drunk to care. She went after him and grabbed onto his arm. She pulled him backwards, ignoring the pain in her ankle, trying to remove him from her home. "You are not welcome here." She grunted with the failed effort. He continued in and settled himself on her furs, his weight on his elbow as he laid back. His legs were sprawled out in front of him.

"I do not care. And perhaps you will change your mind once you have heard what I have to tell you."

She started to say something but Bjarke rose his hand to cut her off. He placed the cup on the floor away from him. "I'm too drunk. I will lose focus. Listen to me and you can speak when I am finished."

She let out a sigh of exasperation as she put her hands on her hips. She shut her mouth and stared at the stubborn, drunken Viking on her floor.

"I," he started as his eyes closed. It was as if he had to find the power to speak. "I dream about you. I think about you. I crave you. I am driven mad day and night because you will not leave my thoughts. I wish... you were by my side instead of her." His eyes opened to look at her and she felt her knees weaken. She swallowed hard as she forced herself to be strong.

"Bjarke. The Gods have cursed me and they told the Seer to warn you. The Seer found me and told me. I kept it from you, I did not want you to worry. But maybe I should have told you. If we marry you will meet the same fate. Maybe even if we do not marry, I will kill you. I am the Raven that lurks over you. I am death for you. I love you and I do not want to kill you." She clenched her fists at her sides and held her breath as she realized she had spoken the words she had kept buried in her heart aloud.

He tilted his head and regarded her as if she'd just confessed that she were a woman instead of her deepest feelings. "Why did you not tell me of the vision before now?"

She avoided his eyes as she crossed her arms under her chest. "I did not wish to worry you about it."

He chuckled as he laid back, when she peeked up his eyes were on her. "You did not tell me because you did not want me to kill you. Did you really think I would be able to do such a thing? To you?"

"You are a great leader, you are generous, you can be kind. You provide everything you can to those around you. You are a good man. But yes, if there is a threat to your family, I do expect you would kill me if I were the threat."

Bjarke extended his hand out to her as if he wanted her to come to him. "It is true. I love you."

"That does not matter now." She refused his hand and watched as he sat up and reached out further.

"It does matter. It will always matter. You will always have my heart, Dalla. Tonight I just wish to lie with the one I love. Odin may call me to Valhalla and I do not wish to leave without first showing you how deep my love for you is."

His fingers brushed hers as she stared at them. He was not going to force her. He was not going to bully her into something she did not want. And she did want him. Slowly his fingers slid up to her wrist, he held it gently, his thumb softly brushing the sensitive flesh over her veins. "Please, Dalla."

She searched over his face all while feeling her resolve weakening. The pull of this man on her was almost too much. "You are drunk."

"I am, very," he said while his eyes locked on hers. "Lie with me, Dalla. Please." His thumb continued to run along her skin.

She glanced towards the doorway, wondering if she had the strength to limp away from him. She felt him tug on her wrist and her eyes went back to him. His lust-filled gaze called to her louder than any words could have. She slowly got down onto the floor with him. Their bodies slowly came closer and closer together as she laid beside him, her hand on his chest where he'd placed it.

His arm slid under her and cradled her against him, his hand sliding up into her black hair. For a long moment he just stared into her eyes. "You are so beautiful, shieldmaiden." His head gradually dipped forward and his lips pressed to hers.

The soft seduction of the kiss sent a jolt of energy through her veins. She wished to tear his clothes from him but she did not want to miss the rest of the kiss. She let him drink from her lips as she tucked the memory into her heart. She knew this could not happen again. She knew he only came here because he had lost his inhibitions. She knew she should walk away before she let herself be hurt.

Her hand went into his hair and pulled him closer as he turned his body into hers. His lips left hers to sear a path down her neck and shoulders. She clung to him as his beard added to the experience, sending sparks of desire through her with each scraggly caress. She moaned softly as his lips re-captured hers, more demanding this time.

As the kiss deepened, she felt his hand start to slide under her clothing to loosen it. Soon her shoulder was bare and then her chest. His tongue glided between her lips as his hand slid over her swollen breast, which ached for his touch, his fingers tracing along it and fingering her nipple to make it erect.

She arched her back and heard him groan as his body moved over hers and he took his place between her legs.

His hips started to move, pressing his growing erection against her center through their clothing as his head moved down to take her hardened nipple into his mouth. She gasped as the thrill of his hot wet mouth rolled through her. She bucked her hips against his, wanting the friction, craving what only he could give her.

"Bjarke, please...," she begged. She angled her head to the side as he pulled his head away to look up at her. He sat back on his knees and untied the strings to his pants. His thumbs disappeared as he shifted them down past his hips. His big hands proceeded to clear the clothing that covered her lower half. Once they were both ready, he lowered himself until he was on top of her and his mouth took possession of hers.

She cried out against his lips as he sunk deep inside of her, slowly. He stilled for a moment, his breath softly playing on her lips. She opened her eyes and looked at him. He was staring back at her. With eyes open, unfaltering, he withdrew from her.

"I love you, Dalla. I want this moment to last for eternity."

She tried to look away as his words tortured her soul, but his thumb pushed her back. She stared into his eyes as he slowly filled her up again. She whimpered as she clung to the backs of his arms as he withdrew and filled her again. Staring into his eyes with him inside of her and sweet words dripping from his lips she suddenly started to panic. Perhaps this was the moment. Perhaps now was the time to tell him that the babe inside of her was his.

"Bjarke, there is something I need to--" She gasped as he slammed into her.

"Do not ruin this with words. I want to hear you moan. I want to hear you say my name, shieldmaiden."

"But Bjarke--" She inhaled sharply again as he thrust hard, her eyes closing to savor the sweet pain that somehow brought the best pleasure.

"You are almost there. I can feel it in the way you clench around me and how you drip." His teeth grazed the curve of her neck sending shivers through her body. She clung to him tighter as he picked up the speed of their lovemaking.

Her moans bounced off the wooden walls as he smirked down at her. She could see the sweat starting to pop out on his forehead from the exertion.

"Say it, Dalla," he grunted as he drove into her, his passion rising with each passing second.

The sound of their bodies slapping together rang in her ears, making her wetter, pushing her closer to the edge. "Yes," she moaned as she lifted her legs higher.

He grunted as he paused for a moment to gather her legs against his chest.

The change of angle made him bottom out in her. He pushed

his hips forward as his girth stretched her. "Say it, Dalla," he said again with a little growl. His hips moving at a medium pace.

She pushed up onto her elbows before grabbing his head. She crushed her lips to his to shut him up.

Bjarke's hands moved under her as he reclined on his knees. He pulled her up with her legs on either side of him and held her onto his cock. His arms gave her no choice but to accept him inside of her over and over again.

She quickly broke the kiss as she got lost in the exquisite feeling of him moving deep inside of her.

His fingers dug into her ass and held her onto him. She tried to lift her hips but his grip stayed true. She cried out in disappointment and disbelief.

"Please!" She bit his lower lip, none too gently.

His growl answered her before his words. "Fucking say it, Dalla and then I will give it to you. I will give it all."

"I love you, Bjarke. Now give it to me!"

His hands at her ass started to push and pull her against his hard thrusts. It hurt, but it felt so good. A moan of pleasure left his lips as he buried his face against her neck and took a bite of the tender flesh, sending more pleasure-filled pain deep in her belly.

She held onto the back of his hair, her moans increasing in volume as her orgasm started to creep closer.

"Bjarke, yes! Oh, yes!"

Two more swift thrusts and she was coming around him, her insides squeezing him tightly as her gush of wetness surrounded him. She cried out in pleasure and held him tightly as she shook in his arms. His teeth found her shoulder as he splashed her insides with his seed.

When the calm took over and the aftershocks of sex faded Bjarke laid them both down. He stayed inside of her as he kissed her forehead. "Eternity," he whispered.

She felt tears spring into her eyes as she stared at him.

They would not have eternity. They would only have this night. "I do not care what the Seer has seen, I cannot keep myself away from you," he whispered, his fingers lazily stroking her back.

"Bjarke." She glanced up studied his serious expression. "You are married. You will not come to me again. If you love me you will stay away."

"I will fail in that."

His words swept through her heart, searing it. She cradled herself against his chest which grew wet with her tears. Bjarke's chest rose and fell with his breath. She stayed only long enough to listen to it slow into a deep slumber.

CHAPTER 21

Dalla watched the boats as they faded from view. Not too long after Bjarke was asleep Dalla had taken her leave of the hut. Catrin had gladly accepted her and said nothing over their morning meal.

That afternoon the raiding party had started their voyage on the open sea. They would not stop until they found land and they would not return until they had riches to return with. She had begged the Gods to keep Bjarke safe. She only hoped they would listen.

The horn blew signaling the village's wishes for safe travels. The men aboard the ships did one last wave to their families.

She took one last look at the sea before turning away. She wished she were sailing along with her fellow warriors. She did not like being left behind. She put a hand over the slight swell in her belly. She would not risk the life of this babe and she would spend the rest of her life protecting it from harm.

Before boarding his ship, Bjarke had approached Catrin. What they spoke of she had no idea, but at the end he gave her shoulder a squeeze. Dalla had stared at Bjarke's back hoping he would look at her but he did not. She felt jealousy, guilt, and a host of other things she had not yet sorted out.

On her way back towards her home, she spotted Gerd stepping towards the woods. She had no business going that way and the way she peeked around her as if she were a disobedient child hoping to avoid unwanted eyes gave Dalla pause. What was she up to?

Despite her feelings of the woods and the trouble they brought, Dalla let Gerd have a start before following her.

Dalla snuck through the woods, her eyes on the ground and the leaves as she made her way behind Gerd. From the looks of it, it was not the first time Gerd had come this way. There was clearly a gently beaten path leading the way. She followed the tracks and signs through the woods quietly. Sounds drifted through the trees to her ears and Dalla stopped to listen.

"Mmm. I missed you so." This was Gerd, was she speaking to herself? Dalla stepped closer, hiding behind trees so as not to be spotted in case Gerd was not alone.

She could see through the small patch of trees the back of a man and could vaguely see Gerd in front of him. Gerd was lowering herself to her knees in front of the man. Dalla stared with wide eyes as Gerd swallowed the man's cock. Her moans mingled with the man's and floated through the woods. After the shock wore off Dalla felt the fury clench in her stomach. How dare she by lying with another man, she was the jarl's wife. It was not uncommon for a married man to lie with another, but for a wife to lie with another? It was not heard of, nor accepted. Divorce was easy enough to acquire. Without thinking she marched forward and just as she reached the couple she called out, "You traitorous whore!"

When her eyes met with the man's she felt her stomach bottom out. A cold sweat broke out on her forehead as she felt the warmth leave her face and her knees begin to weaken. It could not be. She blinked and blinked again and yet it was still him. She knew the woods held bad things. She knew better than to go into them. She was shocked as she stared at him — the man who had given her so much pain as a child. The man she had run from and dreamt of killing nearly every moon while she slept.

"Hello, sister." His voice sent cold shivers through her body as Gerd stood up and hid behind him. He didn't bother to pull up his pants. It was nothing he hadn't forced Dalla to see before. He held his arms open and tilted his head. "Will you not come give your brother a hug? It has been so long."

She took a step backward as her eyes moved from Gerd to Dyri, her older brother. "Wh-what are you doing here?" In an instant she was transformed from a strong shieldmaiden to a petrified six-year-old girl.

"I am going to make love to my woman," he said as his hand moved to his member. As he stroked it she felt bile rising in her throat. "Would you care to watch? Or join us?" One of his dark brows rose in mocking question as his lips upturned in amusement at her discomfort and fear.

A tree behind her stopped her from retreating further, she reached behind her and grabbed ahold of it, hoping it would bring her the strength she was momentarily lacking.

"She is not your woman, Dyri. She is jarl Bjarke's woman. When he finds out--"

His voice and his steps towards her made her pause, "He will not find out. Who is going to tell him?" He glanced over his shoulder at Gerd who was standing there with her hands clasped in front of her as if she were an innocent bystander. "Are you going to tell him?" She shook her head and then he looked back to Dalla, pinning her to the tree with his gaze. "Are you going to tell him, little sister?"

She wanted to close her eyes, erase his face from her memory but it was burned there and she was too frightened of what would happen if she did close her eyes.

"She is the whore I was telling you about, Dyri."

He paused and stared Gerd. He stopped stroking himself as a smirk broke out on his lips. "Is she?" He studied Dalla for a long moment. "Sister, Gerd tells me you have been a very bad girl. You are fucking a married woman's husband?"

She opened her mouth to speak but the words would not come out.

"It's okay, Dalla. I know these things are hard to speak of. You never did like to admit when you had done something wrong. Perhaps we should just move straight to the punishment, shall we? I have missed it."

He closed the distance between them and pressed his shaft against her belly. As his face came closer to hers she turned away, still clinging to the tree.

"I will not punish you today. But if I find out that you have spilled this little secret I will punish you harder than I ever have before. You are a woman now, Dalla. There are things your body can take now that it couldn't before."

She groaned in displeasure when his lips pressed a kiss to her cheek.

"Go back to the village and mind your own home, Dalla. Keep your nose out of mine."

He stepped back and went back to Gerd who got back onto her knees the instant he put his hand on the back of her head.

With the eyes of the serpent off of her she released the tree and darted off into the woods, her ankle singing its angry chorus as she forced it to take her running body. It seemed that the further away she went the more the sounds of her brother's manhood in Gerd's throat echoed in her ears. She could hold her stomach no longer and bent over, retching onto the ground. She sobbed softly as she spit a couple of times.

Gerd did not deserve Bjarke. She would do nothing yet, she was not strong enough and there were no warriors to help her, but once Bjarke returned she would speak of it. Her brother and Gerd would not get off scot free behind the jarl's back. Dalla would make sure of it.

CHAPTER 22

FALL

Bjarke's lips turned into a wide grin as soon as he spotted the familiar flag billowing in the breeze in the distance. The ships rocked on the waves and were full with gold and silver treasures. Only a few warriors who had left did not return. They were in Valhalla and already drunk in celebration. The celebration for Bjarke's men's return would have to wait until the moon rose. It would take at least that long for all the treasures to be brought to the Great Hall and sorted through. The details of the feast, the raid, and his home had been the only things he had thought about on their journey.

Gradually the crowd of women, children, and the elderly gathered on the shore to watch their boats pull back in. As the men jumped out and pulled the boats ashore, the crowds came forward, speaking their praises and their congratulations on a safe journey back home.

Bjarke was one of the last to step off the ship and by then the crowds had moved along with the others as they carried chest after chest of gold and silver towards the Great Hall.

His heart seized in his chest when he laid eyes on Dalla. Many moons he had been gone. Many moons he had dreamt of her, vividly, only to wake covered in sweat and aching. Despite trying to forget her she'd stayed with him. His own version of torture.

Dalla's belly was swollen and her skin seemed to glow as she stood there wrapped in an extra fur. She had never been more beautiful. He pulled his gaze away; it was not his child in her belly, nor her body he would be sleeping next to as the winter took over the weather.

He looked up again, searching for his bride. His brow furrowed as he struggled to lay eyes on her but at last he spotted her, lazily walking down towards the water. She stopped beside Dalla and spoke something into her ear. He noted the red in Dalla's cheeks. What had transpired since he had been gone?

He stepped up to Gerd and wrapped an arm around her in greeting. "Hello, Wife. I have returned with many riches for you."

She grinned as she met his eyes, "And I have already picked out which treasures we will be wearing this moon as we celebrate your return."

His cock did not jump as it should have. He glanced at Dalla who was still standing there. He nodded to her politely before pushing Gerd towards the Great Hall to join the others.

He felt Dalla's eyes on his back but he ignored them and the urge to turn around and run towards her. She was not his wife. Nor his shieldmaiden. Nor his friend. She was not his anything now. He ignored the sinking feeling in his gut and pulled Gerd tighter into his side.

"Tell me everything that has happened since I have been gone."

The feast was nearly ready and Bjarke's stomach grumbled in appreciation as the smell of roasted hog filled the large room. Already people were milling around and taking their seats. And already Bjarke had twice filled his cup.

Gerd had spoken more words in a few hours than he had heard muttered the entire length of the raid. The only way he would be able to be merry this eve was to drown himself ever so slightly in mead. As was his right. He was celebrating the good fortune the Gods had shown them.

He was growing bored waiting for everyone to arrive so he could give his speech. His mind drifted in and out between Dalla and what he must say to his people. Finally the horn sounded, signaling the start of the feast, and he stood.

"The Gods granted us much. They shielded us who they saw fit and took the others to Valhalla where they drink now. We shall drink with them in memory. Our coffers are full, we have food for the winter, and now we feast! All is well my brothers and sisters. Come. Let us celebrate."

He lifted his cup and drained it dry before sitting down once more. A thrall, whose name he could no longer remember, placed food in front of him and he filled his belly. He was barely halfway through his meal when he noticed a hand slide across his inner thigh. He glanced down at it and then followed the limb upwards. Gerd. He smiled a little. He leaned over and spoke into her ear.

"I nearly forgot we were supposed to touch each other in front of the eyes of others."

The beginning of a smile tipped her lips. "I am merely doing what I am supposed to. Especially after my husband has been gone so long overseas." Her hand dipped closer to his balls, clouding his mind as the blood rushed to his cock. He had been too long without a woman.

He grabbed onto her hand and pushed it back down to his knee. "You may stop now."

She continued to smile though her voice dripped ice. "Perhaps I do not wish to. Perhaps I wish to punish you for fucking Dalla and yelling out for all to hear that you love her."

He frowned as her words moved through his brain. He gripped her wrist to keep her hand from moving any further. "You are mistaken, Wife."

She snatched her hand back and used it to smooth her hair from her face. "I am not."

He frowned and shook his head, picking his food up again. The woman was mad, clearly. He may have fucked Dalla and maybe he even felt something beyond lust for her, but he would never have spoken those words aloud. He had never spoken those words to anyone save for his mother and his sister and that was a different love. Not even the same word.

He ripped the meat with his teeth roughly as he looked around the hall. Where the hell was she? He thought if he could just see her face that it would confirm that he had not claimed something as ridiculous as love for her. Finally he located her, almost out the door, surrounded by shield-maidens and friends. All women. And yet she looked so alone. Their eyes met, and he flinched as the sparks traveled immediately to his belly. His eyes ripped away from hers and looked down at his plate, nearly empty.

"Did she say it back?" he asked just before putting the cup to his lips.

Gerd turned towards him and grabbed his head. She held him still while she kissed him publicly. His poor cock was more confused now than it had ever been. Some mead splashed from his cup and onto his clothing. He pulled away from the kiss with a growl. She smiled at him. "You think I stayed to listen? How very misguided of you, Husband."

He stared at his food once more. He looked at her retreating backside when he felt her warmth moving away from him. She was lying. He knew she was lying. There was only one way to find out for sure. His eyes went back to Dalla. He knew she would not lie to him.

Dalla was still among the shieldmaidens as Bjarke filled his half spilled cup to full again. Most of it was drunk down before one of the warriors approached him and started making idle chit chat about the next raid which was still too many moons away to consider. After a few minutes the warrior moved off and when Bjarke's eyes searched for Dalla, he couldn't find her.

The rest of the mead was finished, and he stood from his seat at the head of the hall. Not many looked in his direction. They were too busy drinking and celebrating with words and laughter. He stepped outside into the cool air, the mead moving through his system and clouding his mind just slightly.

He caught sight of Dalla's dress just as she disappeared between two longhouses. He smiled to himself as he walked that way with purpose. Did she wish to be followed? Was she disappearing on purpose so that he would find her? It did not matter. He was determined to get answers about Gerd's accusation.

Those thoughts of getting answers soon turned to thoughts of her swollen breasts pressed against his chest, and the sounds of her moans tickling his ears. The feeling of her insides clamped around him. Lost in his thoughts, he'd moved closer to the woods without notice. He groaned and rubbed his swelling member with his hand as he paused beside a tree. He needed to sink into her soon or he was going to go mad. Madder.

The sound of Dalla's voice carrying through the trees brought his attention back to the present. He furrowed his brow as he stepped as quietly as he could towards the noise. She sounded angry, and it left him wondering what she would be doing in the woods alone. Was she mad? Speaking with herself aloud? As he got closer, the words became clearer, and he paused, listening.

CHAPTER 23

She pointed a finger at Dyri who stood with his arms crossed in the middle of the small clearing. "You need to stay away from her, brother. I am no longer afraid of you. You are right, I have grown up. I have grown into a strong shield-maiden and I will no longer allow you to threaten me or my family."

He smiled though his eyes gleamed darkly. "You should still be afraid of me, dear little sister."

"But I am not. Stay away from her or I will stick you through your guts and leave you here with them draped from your body, food for the hungriest predator in these woods."

His arms uncrossed and hung by his sides as he stepped forward a step. "Such big words. For a moment I almost believed them. Tell me, why all of a sudden have you decided you will not hold your tongue? What did he do? He is back now from his pillaging as she said, isn't he?"

She stayed where she was, not backing down, not cowering from him any longer. "He did nothing but love his wife. His wife, Dyri. Not yours. He is going to have a family with her, not you. Why must you always desire the unattainable?"

A grin moved along his lips. "Because I can," his voice dropped to barely a whisper. "Do you think their babes will come out with hair like hers? Or will they come out with hair like mine?"

She frowned as he took another step towards her, his hand reaching out towards her hair.

"It does not matter what color hair the children have. He is the jarl and you, you are nothing. Gerd will not leave him because he has something you do not. Power. Riches. Respect," she spat.

She gritted her teeth as he grabbed a chunk of her hair tightly and yanked. "Stupid." Dyri said as spittle splashed on her cheek. "Do you not think we have a plan? We have been planning and plotting the death of her father for years. Bjarke took care of Torg for us. But it still did not work out. She was here and alone and a stranger. And now that she has Bjarke wrapped around her finger I can finally come into the fold, gain his trust. Gain everyone's trust and when the time is right I will challenge him and take what should have always been mine."

With her head tilted to the side, still tightly in his grasp, she narrowed her eyes, "You are the stupid one. Leave now or I will end you. Leave now and you will get to keep your body. Leave now and maybe you will still have the chance to live the next life in Valhalla."

Her body jerked violently as he pulled her towards him and then pushed. The force which she hit the tree behind her took the wind from her. She also heard something crack and felt the pain in her chest. She grunted, her vision darkening as the pain claimed her. She forced her eyes back open as her brother stood over her hunched body. He would not be smiling soon. She moved slowly around the tree and reached for her sword which she had hidden from him. She winced as she pulled it along the ground towards her.

He laughed when he saw it. "Look at you, little sister. That is not a toy. Do not be foolish."

She gripped the metal in her hand tightly, took a deep breath and made a quick slash at him. He was able to jump back almost in time, her sword slashed through his right hand.

With a growl of pain her brother came right in at her as she tried to bring her sword back up. His boot connected with her swollen stomach and sent her back into the tree. The pain moved through her as the wind left her again. It was hard to breathe between the pain in her chest and the pain in her stomach.

Again her brother stood over her and pulled the sword from her hand. It looked as if he was going to kill her. "You should not act so defiant little sister. Remember, I will always be your big br--," his words were cut short. In her eyes before she had to close them it looked like a wild animal sprung upon Dyri, but she heard the grunts and thuds and knew it was Bjarke. He had followed her.

She tried to sit herself up, but the pain was too great. From the ground she watched as they tumbled and wrestled. Bjarke was a great warrior but for some reason he could not manage to get the upper hand. She closed her eyes and groaned as her stomach contracted. It was worse than any pain she had ever felt, tears sprung to her eyes and she was rendered speechless for a long moment.

When she opened her eyes, she saw Bjarke raining blows

down upon her brother who somehow managed to get out of his grasp and struggle to his feet and into the woods. Bjarke rose as if to give chase, but her cry of pain made him stop as he turned towards her. The fear and panic in his eyes was enough to punch a hole in her heart. Something was wrong. Terribly wrong. She had only seen that look on his face once before when he was holding his dying brother in his arms on the battlefield.

She cried out again as her body squeezed with pain. Bjarke's strong arms were around her as he lifted her and held her gently against his large chest, still panting from the fight with Dyri. She barely noticed that he smelled of sweat and mead as another one gripped her.

"Shh, Dalla. We will find you a healer. You will not go to Valhalla today."

Each step he took was blinding as pain gripped her tighter and harder. She held her breath to keep from crying out and the last thing she remembered was his voice.

"Do not leave me."

CHAPTER 24

Bjarke was almost to Catrin's home. Her blood was dripping onto the ground from his elbow, leaving a trail behind him. Others who saw him followed and by the time he pushed through Catrin's door there were at least fifty eyes on them. "Catrin!" He somehow managed to get words out past the constriction in his throat as he looked around. Catrin was already coming towards him, concern in her eyes. Bjarke laid Dalla down onto Catrin's furs.

"What happened?" Catrin gasped.

"A man with dark hair attacked her in the woods. He called her sister. Do not leave her side. I must get word to the Hraun." He turned around and left the house.

"My jarl there is no need to get word to Hraun…" Catrin's words faded as Bjarke pushed through the crowd.

"Do not stand here! Do not watch her die! Men! Gather your weapons, search the woods for a man with black hair. Do not return here until you find him. The wounds on his face will tell you it is him. Bring him back here to me. Alive. You!" He grabbed a lanky village boy by the shoulder and stared him in the eye. Catrin's word finally reached his ears and he swung around to face her. "Why is there no need to get work to Hraun? Is Kol not the father?"

Catrin twisted her hands in front of her, not meeting his eyes. "No, my jarl."

"Who is the father then, Catrin? Is it that bastard, Sokki?"

Catrin lifted her head and opened her mouth to speak. The fury in his eyes stopped her from saying anything and Bjarke took that to confirm that Sokki was indeed the father. He turned back to the lanky boy. "Go find Sokki. Tell him to come here. Immediately. His jarl commands it."

Everyone dispersed soon after he issued his orders, all except one. The healer. He grabbed onto her arm and pulled the elderly lady into Catrin's house.

Sokki had arrived, out of breath, and stood back, one arm folded over his chest, the other on his lips as he observed the scene. "What happened?" Sokki did not move closer. Bjarke felt his jaw clenching in rage. Why was he not moving to be beside her in her time of need? Could he not see his child was dying inside of her?

"A man with dark hair attacked her in the woods. He called her sister. Do not leave her side. Pretend you are distraught that she may be close to death. And pretend that the loss of your child weighs heavy in your heart." He turned around, unable to lay eyes upon Sokki any longer.

Catrin took a seat beside her friend. Dalla's face was paler than the freshly fallen snow.

"Heal her!" he snarled as he moved out of the home which was too small. He paced in front of Catrin's home as he waited. He did not know what he would do if Dalla did not live. He could not even think of it. The only thing he could think was that she did not belong on the floor of her friend's home, she belonged in the Great Hall with him.

He ran his fingers through his hair in distress. He waited for what felt like an eternity as the scene he had stumbled upon replayed in his mind. As soon as he'd seen Dalla swing her sword Bjarke had come running. And yet he hadn't been fast enough. Twice she had needed him and he hadn't been there.

The sun was starting to rise when finally the healer came out from the longhouse. "My jarl, I have done all that I can." For a moment his heart seized in his chest and his guts dropped to his knees before she continued, "Freya, the goddess, took the child. The mother must rest now."

He nodded his head and waited until she was out of sight to run his hand over his face in relief. Tears pricked at his eyes as he shook his head. He would not cry. He was not weak. He stared at the morning sky and said a silent thank you to the Gods for not taking Dalla to Valhalla.

Catrin cleared her throat and when Bjarke swung around Catrin was standing just behind him, her arms crossed over her chest. "I am so sorry, my jarl."

"Just take care of her, Catrin." Bjarke's voice almost cracked, but he cleared his throat.

"Jarl, there is something you must know," Catrin started and paused, "I wish it could come from her own lips. Dalla… That babe…" The silence held in the air for a long moment. "It was not any other man's, but yours. I am so sorry to say it jarl Bjarke."

His shoulders rolled as he listened to the words of Catrin.

Had he heard her right? "You mean to tell me that no other man had eyes on her, nor ever lain with her?"

Catrin nodded his head to Bjarke as his eyes looked back at the longhouse. Knowing that he was the father he felt ashamed for keeping himself outside. His eyes turned to Catrin, and she immediately shrunk under the weight of them. "You let me believe that Sokki was the father. He stood by and watched a woman he had no feelings for wrestle with death? I would not want the likes of you as a friend."

His fists tightened at his side as he turned away from Catrin. The Gods had chosen to bless him with a child with the woman he found irresistible, and now to find out it had been taken away... Fury and resentment coursed through his blood. He could not help but wonder why she had not told him the child in her belly was hers. His anger was turning on her as he realized that the death was partly her fault. Had she told him the truth about the pregnancy he could have protected her, he would have done anything in his powers to protect her. He would have stayed by her side, made sure she had the finest longhouse, the finest food. His heart was now ripped into pieces. He had lost a child. And this may have been his only chance.

Catrin sniffled at his harsh words, but spoke hers softly. "Did you wish to see your daughter? She is tiny but... but still your daughter, your blood."

The knuckles of Bjarke's fists whitened with the strain of how forceful he held them closed. Again he felt the tears prick at his eyes. For a moment he thought of bouncing a little girl on his lap, would he regret never seeing her face? If he did not see her face now how would he know her when he joined her in Valhalla, for surely that is where she would be.

"Yes," Bjarke choked out as he turned. "Bring her to me." He did not wish to see Dalla's face. His chest squeezed tightly as he replayed her treachery in his mind.

Catrin moved inside and after a few moments brought a bundle of furs out to him. He took them and at first he thought Catrin had forgotten his daughter, the furs were light. Slowly and with shaking fingers he opened it. There amongst the gray was his tiny daughter, still pink with blood, and thin because she did not have enough time to grow fat inside of her mother's womb. His finger stroked along her cheek. It looked so large comparatively. That is when the tears fell from his eyes. He touched every inch of her tiny body from the top of her head to her curled up fists to her toes. Though his throat was tight, he managed a few words. "I cannot wait to be with you again, Inga." The rest of his words were choked by his tears. He covered the body and handed the furs back to Catrin and turned. He couldn't be there any longer. Not with his daughter he could not watch grow older or with her mother, who may as well have died too, for she was dead to him for allowing this to happen to his only daughter.

CHAPTER 25

The darkness lifted as she became aware of her body. The pain overpowered her as she tried to move her limbs. The memory of what had happened came rushing back and she let out a soft gasp as she recalled Bjarke, Dyri, the sword. She opened her eyes and was surrounded by darkness. The faint sounds of snores drifted towards her through her panting. She put her head down and moved her hand to her stomach; she had hoped she would waken to feel the babe stirring. Her panting grew louder as panic seized her. Her hand ran over deflated skin.

This could not be true. This must be a dream. She heard screaming, and it wasn't until she felt arms around her that she realized they were her own.

"Dalla, we are here." Someone moved around behind them and Dalla spun her head around to try to see. It was only Catrin, who stoked the fire and put on a new log.

"My baby...?"

"She has gone with Freya, Dalla. jarl Bjarke named her Inga. We made a pyre for her two moons ago while you were still in the darkness."

Gone. Gone. Her baby was gone. She felt as if her heart were being torn in two. She had preferred the feeling of a broken bone inside her chest than this. This pain was deadening. She lost the one thing she had vowed to protect above all else. She was a failure and because of it she would never get to hold her daughter in her arms. Inga. She cried against Catrin and as she cried, she felt it all melt away into nothing. Her baby was gone. She no longer care about herself. About pain. About anything. She felt she would never be able to fill the hole that was now in her heart.

Catrin's hand rubbed her back even as the cries subsided.

"Does he know?" Dalla asked, no longer afraid of the answer. For if he did he would hate her. And if he didn't he would soon hate her when she told him.

Catrin cleared her throat. "Yes. He knows. He is angry. Hurt. Mourning, like you."

She laid down and rolled over, the pain from her rib barely a throb compared to the rest. "Did they find him?"

Again Catrin spoke, "Not yet. But they are searching. And jarl Bjarke wants him dead."

"As do I," she whispered. She felt a warm, gentle hand on her back that moved to her hair.

"Do not worry, Dalla. jarl Bjarke will find him and he will pay for what he did to you."

They did not know the half of what he had done to her. She

closed her eyes against the dim light and tried to fall back asleep. If she were asleep perhaps she could see her daughter's face, touch her skin, smell her hair.

The Gods offered her mercy, she fell asleep. And in her dreams she met her Inga.

CHAPTER 26

A few more days of rest and Dalla was escorted to her own home. As she laid down on her own furs, she sighed in relief. She was finally alone. She could finally mourn in peace. She would no longer have to contain her crying if she did not wish to. The whole of the day was spent on her bed. She stared at the fire, lost in her grief.

Just before nightfall she fell asleep. She was not sure what woke her in the darkest part of night but she thought nothing of it. Perhaps it was just someone outside, stumbling home. She heard the soft sound of breathing as she had a moment to panic before she felt weight press down on her chest. Icy fingers covered her mouth to keep her from screaming.

"Oh, dear sister." Those words chilled her to the bone, but were equaled by the loathing that began to boil in her blood. Her body was sluggish and pained as she struggled. Her brother was too heavy to get him off of her. Much like when she was a child. "Stop struggling. I came to pay you back for cutting my hand. Came to punish you as I used to, but this time... this time you are a woman." His hand clutched her breast roughly. The pain from her rib was sharp with his weight upon her.

"Did you miss me? Did you miss my touch upon your skin? Do you miss me leaving you with more scars?" Dyri chuckled above her as he shifted, his hand still covering her mouth but now he pushed between her legs as his body held her down.

She stilled as she opened her mouth and let her tongue flick across his fingers.

She heard her brother growl and felt him press his hips forward against her clothed center. He was hard, and the tease had worked. As he loosened his fingers on her mouth, she bared her teeth and bit him. The metallic taste of his blood pooled into her mouth as she held on and clenched her teeth together.

She felt his other hand leave her breast as he cursed loudly. "Fucking bitch!" His free hand came across her cheek to try to get her teeth to let go but she only bit down further, her teeth almost fully together with his chunk of flesh between them.

She felt his hand close around her throat, cutting the air from getting inside of her lungs, only then did she let go and gasp for air.

He repositioned himself on top of her as he wrapped his arm around her neck from behind. His muscles restricting her airway to keep her quiet. "You will pay for that, sister." He shuffled, the arm around her tightening and loosening as he moved. She felt cool air on the backs of her legs as he got her skirts up. She struggled to get her hands out from under her body as he pressed his dick against her bottom.

"Gerd does not let me take her here. Only you," he whispered into her ear as his hand grabbed her fleshy cheek and pulled it to the side to expose her hole.

The pain in her chest was growing as she tried to rock her body. Her hand was almost free and time was running out. His breath quivered as he slid his tip over her skin. Just as he pressed it inside of her she freed her arm and thrust her fingers into his eye.

The arm around her neck let go as Dyri fell back away from her. She clawed at the furs, trying to pull her body away from his. She was still too weak and deathly afraid of what would happen when he rose from the floor.

CHAPTER 27

Bjarke tossed and turned on his pallet. Gerd was sleeping soundly beside him, he wondered as he looked at her if she knew about what had happened. Surely she knew that Dalla had lost her child. But did she know that it was his? Did she know that it tormented him? If she did, she pretended not to know.

Bjarke sat up. He pulled himself from the pallet and the sleeping Gerd and got dressed. He did not want to wake her with his restlessness. He adorned a few extra furs and moved through the flap and out into the night. His breath showed in the night air with the chill around him. For the past few days his anger tormented him. When he was awake, he could only think of Dalla and her brother. He wanted her brother to suffer, he wanted to take the breath from his throat. And Dalla... he did not know what to think of her. He was still angry for keeping the secret. But once sleep took him he dreamed of her, of being inside of her, of being a husband to her. The Gods were torturing him and he did not know why. Maybe because he had ignored the message they'd delivered through the Seer. As he walked, he revisited the Seer's words once more.

The bear and his cub are being followed by a Raven.

Clearly the raven was the dark-haired man.

The raven will bring nothing but pain and suffering.

This raven very well sounded like Dalla if he ignored their heated moments together.

He must kill the Raven or it will kill him and those he loves.

Bjarke's jaw tightened as he replayed the last line in his head. Despite trying to find the dark-haired man, Dalla's brother, had eluded him and his men. He would love the opportunity to kill him, but he had not been afforded the chance.

The hands at his side clenched and opened to try to keep the blood flowing through them as they grew cold. The fur boots crunched on the near frozen ground as he walked, his mind clear of anything. It wasn't until his eyes rose that he realized he was standing in front of Dalla's longhouse. Smoke rose from the flue and into the night sky. For a moment he paused there with his eyes locked on the flap of the doorway. He hadn't known she'd moved back into her own home. He considered the possibility for a moment that she wasn't alone and as he turned to walk away, he heard Dalla's weak, strained voice and his heart thundered loudly in his chest.

"Help! Help!" He heard her cough and the struggling within.

His feet swiftly carried him inside, his eyes took in the scene before him. He glanced around and grabbed the nearest weapon he could find. He lifted Dalla's shield into the air and brought it down upon the back of Dyri's skull. The man had no time to react as everything happened so fast. Dyri crumpled and tried to pull himself away from Dalla and Bjarke. The shield was brought down again catching the man's shoulder and face. Dyri curled into a ball and tried to protect himself. The shield was discarded as Bjarke overpowered him on the ground. A few times his fists connected with the man. "You... you ...," He had the man responsible for the death of his daughter below him and there was nothing to stop him. Save for Dalla who was laying there watching him, her face pale, her eyes widened from his fury.

When Dyri did not fight back Bjarke stepped back. Dyri looked up at him. His eye swollen shut from Dalla's fingers and Bjarke's fists. Dyri chuckled as he spoke, lifting himself to a seated position, "Gerd told me of your fury, told me how you were. When you stop laying with a whore, she will seek others to satisfy her. I fucked her, jarl, and I fucked her good. Many moons she called my name and praised the Gods. And my sweet sister, she is the worst kind of woman. So disobedient. So strong-willed."

Bjarke was barely containing himself, his feet bringing him closer to the man with each passing second.

"She used to settle down really well but only after I defiled her most secret hole. It works very well. I know you will kill me. Just promise me that when I am gone, you will show my sister the kind of punishment she deserves. She is too wild. She needs a strong man to keep her tame. And since I know you have already lain with her, I know you are aware."

Further words were cut short by his boot which caused the man's head to jerk back from the impact, sending him back down to the floor. "Shut up," Bjarke said, "Tonight... tonight you die and will not meet with the others in Valhalla." The sword's metal scraped against its sheath as Bjarke grabbed it.

"Please care for my seed growing in Gerd's belly. You will find out soon enough it is not yours."

Bjarke moved behind him and took hold of a hand full of his hair. He pulled him up to face Dalla. "Look at your sister. LOOK AT HER!" Bjarke put the blade to Dyri's neck. "I want her to be the last thing you see before you die."

Dyri chuckled, but it was cut short by the sword that severed his head from his body. The body slumped to the floor, and the head remained held by the hair in Bjarke's hand. He threw the blade on the floor by the body and stood there. He had hoped that Dyri's death would have felt better than this.

"Bjarke..."

"Not now, Dalla! I must plan my next move." He stared at the flames in the fire. A slow drip sounded as Dyri's blood collected on the floor beside his feet.

CHAPTER 28

In the corner of the room he sat. The fire crackled with its last embers. Bjarke had made sure to not add more wood so the fire would go out just as the sun rose. When the chill spread through the air in their home, it caused Gerd to shift under the furs. As the sun rose everything inside shone with a soft golden glow. Bjarke watched as her hand snuck out from under the fur to his side of the bed. Her hand crumpled in the cold spot and her eyes fluttered open. A scream ripped through the air as she realized her hand was on a blood stained fur and the pale face of Dyri, her ex-lover, was in Bjarke's place. The soul gone from his eyes, which had remained open. His mouth was partially closed in a crooked smile.

She jerked back away from the severed head and fell from the pallet on the floor. With a grunt she looked around and saw Bjarke sitting there in the corner of their home within the Great Hall.

"What is this?" she demanded, "What mockery do you play at? Who is this man?"

With a groan he stood from the chair, the blood-stained sword held in his hand with white knuckles. "Don't play dumb with me, whore," he said with a growl.

Gerd became hysterical, tears suddenly escaping from her eyes and falling down her cheeks. "He forced me, husband! He said he would hurt me if I did not and that I couldn't tell you! I'm innocent... I swear to the Gods!" she pleaded.

A laugh came from deep within his belly as he moved towards her. He grabbed her by her hair as her hands rose to grab his wrist. He pulled her out into the roads of the village kicking and screaming. In the center of the town was the smith where they forged their weapons. It would be there he hauled her and tied her to a post.

People were starting to gather to watch as the noise drew them from their homes like wolves surrounding a dying animal.

Gerd was screaming for help but no one moved to aid her. Bjarke moved over and pulled one of the brands they used for their cattle. It was sitting within the forge and glowed orange with skin-melting heat.

"What... what are you going to do? I am with child, Bjarke, please!" Gerd's quivering voice begged.

Bjarke moved towards her with the brand held by gloved hand. "But not with my child," he said to her as he pressed the brand against the skin of her chest. She screamed in terror and pain as the brand sizzled, forever marking her. "You have lied, Wife. You were conspiring to take the village from me."

She whimpered against the ground when he released the brand and tossed it away. "I only wanted..." She paused when he got down onto his knee and came close to her face.

"What, my wife? What did you want?"

"I only wanted to protect you. From that woman."

Bjarke scoffed as he drew the blade from his belt. Gerd's eyes grew wide as she looked at the blade and then up at him.

"PLEASE!" she screamed, hysterical and wild, pulling against her restraints. "The Seer told me to protect you from the raven, jarl! She is the raven!" The sobs escaped her throat as she continued to struggle.

"The raven showed itself when it caused the death of my babe within Dalla's belly. The raven was the man with black hair who planned with you to challenge me and take what is mine." His hands opened and motioned to the village around them.

She shook her head. "No. No, no, I swear. It is her. The Seer spoke with me. Shared with me. We were going to move your gold so that she could not steal it. We were going to move away so that your son could live. Please," she cried, her body quivering at his feet as he stood up once more and straddled her back.

His hand moved into her hair and yanked her head back. She screamed as the hair was cut near the scalp of her head and tossed to the ground. Then his hand took hold of her sniveling face and drew the point of the dagger along each cheek.

"I mark you in disgrace. I divorce you, Gerd, in front of my people and the Gods. You are no longer my wife. From this day forward others shall see these marks and know of what you did. And from this day forward you are no longer allowed to live on my lands. You will be banished from this one and any other I may conquer. If I see you again I will kill you. And your babe. You are blessed by the Gods that I have mercy upon you now."

Blood trickled down her cheeks from the wounds as she cried. He sliced the ties binding her to the post and pointed his blade at her throat. "Do not collect your things. You have nothing except what is on your back and in your belly."

He watched as she stumbled away. He knew she would be fine. She would use her body, what was left of it, to seduce a farmer or a fisherman into taking her into his home. He clenched his jaw as the villagers stared at him. He still had a mess to clean up, but he had no idea how to go about it. He slid his blade back into his belt and walked off towards the Great Hall. First, he would need to burn the furs tainted by his late wife. After that he was not so sure.

CHAPTER 29

Catrin visited Dalla daily within her longhouse and brought her food so her strength would return on its own. While she visited, she made sure she mentioned Bjarke at least once though more often than not it was all she talked about while trying to pretend it wasn't strictly for Dalla's benefit. Dalla, on the other hand, said little. Her heart was still healing from everything that had happened. She was still ashamed that she had not been the one to murder Dyri. It was her he had wronged and it should have been her hand on the sword, but she had been too weak.

She still woke in a sweat every evening as the nightmare she'd lived came back in her dreams. Some nights it was Dalla who killed him, some nights she was never rescued and the best nights Bjarke held her after slitting Dyri's throat.

She longed to see Bjarke. Every sunset she hoped it would be him walking into her home instead of Catrin. Every evening she was disappointed.

Three weeks after Gerd's exile, Dalla finally had the strength and the courage to eat her meal in the Great Hall. Catrin had said there was a great buzz in the village and that an announcement would be made over a feast.

Indeed, she was correct, there were excited faces and furious conversation as she moved through the crowds to claim herself a seat. She looked up to the spot where Bjarke should have been but it was empty. She wondered if he was going to claim another bride. It was one of the many rumors floating around and the only one that had her gut churning in disapproval, or maybe it was fear.

Sokki and Catrin joined her at the table. "Dalla, you look a bit less like death," Sokki teased her, offering her a grin.

"Oh, yes. Thank you. You look... the same, I am sorry to say," she shot back, the tiniest of smiles at the corner of her lips.

"I would be offended but I know your tastes are unusual." Sokki's smile faded as he realized the error of his words and quickly he spoke to try to minimize the bite. But the damage had already been done and Dalla felt her guts twisting again. "Do you think he will be sending villagers to Beckby?" It was another of the rumors going around and Sokki was clearly trying to distract her with it.

"I do not even pretend to know what the jarl may be about. I am sure whatever it is, it will be the best choice. He does not make mistakes."

Catrin put her hand on Dalla's and squeezed. "He does. He is but a man."

Dalla nodded and looked away as the horn blew. Bjarke was standing at his seat. Her eyes drank him up as he stood there, so strong and powerful. He had aged slightly since they had returned in the spring. But it did not make him any less attractive. The crinkles on his brow and the slight silver in his hair made him appear wiser. And she had no doubt that he was. He had lost much. So much. Sorrow filled her heart now as he began to speak.

"It has been twenty and one moons since our village was freed from the plague that was dropped into our midst from the late Jarl Torg, his daughter, Gerd. It will take many more moons for our hearts to heal and our swords to sharpen. Winter is coming quickly upon us and we cannot raid ," the voices in the halls turned despondent at his words but he held his hands up with a solemn expression, giving them pause, "but we will have a battle to fight. A battle that may leave many of us eating in the noisy halls of Valhalla when the flowers begin to bloom."

He looked around the room, meeting eyes with everyone. Everyone but her. Still he avoided her gaze, and she felt the disappointment coursing through her. She had hoped he would have forgiven her. She had hoped that they would be able to come together. She was a fool.

"Our brothers and sisters across the narrow water in Beckby have not had a prosperous year. Most are sick, elderly. They need our help or they will die. It is because of this that I ask for volunteers to pack up their lives here and settle there. You will be rewarded for your loyalty and your good will. It is a chance to start afresh. If you wish to set sail and make the journey which will not take but a few days, then I ask you meet the boats at the shore at sunrise tomorrow. We will send supplies to bolster theirs until their farms and livestock can be harvested and replenished."

People started to talk around the hall. This was a big announcement indeed and one most didn't think would come. Dalla herself was lost in thought as the food was passed between hands. She did not wish to travel by sea, necessarily, but it was torture for her to be so close to Bjarke and feel as if she were dead to him. She had been wrong about the message from the Seer, she knew that now. She had wasted time pushing him away from her. She knew the reason they were not together was her fault and her fault alone. She had damaged them and she saw no other recourse. She ate her food, the taste not registering on her tongue, as she took inventory of what she would take with her to her new life.

Dalla looked to Catrin, "Will you come with me?"

They gazed at each other and something passed between them before turning their eyes to her, "Are you sure you wish to go?" Sokki asked.

"Yes, I am sure. There is nothing left for me here except pain and terrible memories. I am ready to make new ones. Happier ones."

Catrin reached out and clasped Dalla's hand. "Of course I will go with you. I am your dearest friend," Catrin confirmed with a smile.

Dalla nodded her head as her defenses lowered a little and the confidence in her decision settled on her. "I will leave to pack then. I will see you in the morning."

Catrin smiled softly just before Dalla turned away and headed for the doorway. She looked over her shoulder at the villagers, the Great Hall, and Bjarke, one last time before turning away again. She would miss it, all of it, but it was the right decision.

Halfway through her trunk being packed she felt eyes upon

her. When she turned she saw a large figure standing inside of her doorway. He was too damned large to be so quiet. This was the first time he had made eye contact with her since the loss of their child.

Her heart, which she thought was forever broken, started to come to life in her chest as she stared into his icy sea-form colored eyes.

"You are leaving?" His deep voice rang through the small room. The tone was different. A mix of surprise and anguish mingled in his words.

She turned away to hide her expression and the thrill she felt that he seemed to care either way. "I am. I think it would be best."

"I don't," he said plainly.

What did he mean by that? She busied her hands in her furs as her insides squeezed at his words.

"No?" She tried to sound as if she did not care, the quiver gave her away.

She heard his feet carry him closer to her. "No, I don't. " There was a long moment before anything was said. Just as she started to speak he cut her off. "Stay. Stay with me."

She closed her eyes as her body froze. She wanted to remember those words. She wanted to roll in them. She turned around to face him, she felt the hot burn of tears in her eyes. "I am so sorry."

He must have thought she was telling him she would not stay, his face dropped in disappointment. "Is there nothing I can do to convince you that your place is here with me?"

She smiled and shook her head. Again he took her actions as

rejection and did not give her time to finish before he shut her down and turned away. She clutched the furs to her chest as she called out to him, "Bjarke! I am sorry for hurting you. Our child."

It was his turn to stop. Gradually he turned around and his eyes met hers. "Her name was Inga. She was beautiful."

She nodded and peered down at the floor. "Yes. Inga. I only hope one day I will be able to see her."

"I took in every detail. Follow me in Valhalla and I will lead you to her."

The pain of the loss was still so raw. Before she could stop them, the tears started to flow from her eyes. She covered them and let them go when she felt his arms wrap around her and comfort her. She wished he could have done this before. She had missed him so. For the moment they mourned together. She thought she'd never feel this feeling again. The feeling of him and her together.

She wrapped her arms around him and cried against his chest. She had been so alone and now she had some closure. He had forgiven her for what she had done. Forgiven her her lies. She could feel it between them. He still loved her. And she... she had finally allowed herself to let him love her.

Bjarke's hand moved to her head and pulled her away from his chest, turning her face up to look at him. His thumbs wiped away the tears that ran down her cheeks in the same moment that she wiped away his. "Stay with me, Dalla. Let me show you for the rest of our lives how sorry I am for what has happened between us."

"Does this mean you love me?" she asked in a whisper, her voice still thick with tears.

His eyes searched hers. "I did not think I would ever admit to having those feelings. But I do, Dalla. I love you. For as long as I live. And after."

"I will love you longer," she proclaimed just before his passion broke and hungrily shut her up with his lips.

"I will never tire of you. You are my match, Dalla. My equal. You are perfect, my shieldmaiden."

CHAPTER 30

THREE MONTHS LATER...

Bjarke's lips traced a line from Dalla's shoulder to just behind her ear, waking her. His hand came to settle on the gentle roundness of her belly as he snuggled himself closer to her backside.

Dalla's lips curled into a smile. "It is too early, Bjarke."

"Nay. The skies are waking the birds. Do you not hear it?" He rubbed her slightly swollen tummy, only the two of them knew of the life growing inside of her. Soon they would no longer be able to hide it. He took her earlobe between his lips and let a rush of his breath tickle her ear. As he'd intended she laughed and writhed against him, curling in on herself. She pressed her hand to his chin and pushed him away.

"It is too early," she repeated, putting her hand on top of his.

"Mm." Gently he let his hand slide down between her thighs. His teeth nipped at her shoulder. She gasped in surprise as his finger slid over her tender cleft. "Is my shieldmaiden certain it is too early?"

She groaned and grabbed onto his wrist. Turning slightly she draped her leg over his. "Now it is not."

Bjarke chuckled as he teased the woman he loved. When he was laying with her there was nothing else that clouded his thoughts, it was only her.

Slowly his drenched finger entered her opening. She hissed with pleasure, her hips rising to accept him.

The horn blew outside, signaling boats on the horizon.

Dalla's fingers around Bjarke's wrist tightened and she lifted her head, looking towards the flap of their quarters.

Bjarke paid no mind, if it were urgent it would sound again. And if ships were coming, it meant he would soon have visitors and he would no longer be able to do things to his woman.

He slipped from behind her and quickly moved between her legs. She sat up and kept him at bay with her feet. "Bjarke…"

He looked at her with a frown. "Dalla, my love. Please?"

She laughed, trying to cover it with a frown. "Later. We must see who is approaching. What if it's Torg's men? Come to get revenge?"

"Beckby pledged to me."

"You can never be sure. Not all men honor their word as you do."

He growled and rose from their furs. "Now I will be grouchy all day. All of Asar will have you to thank for that."

She smiled as she pulled her skirt down and rose. Before he could slip away she wrapped her arms around his shoulders and pulled him in for a kiss. She had nicknamed it the healing kiss. Whenever she gave it to him it seemed to heal any maladies he'd previously had, including grouchiness.

She slipped her hands into his hair and pressed her body fully against his. He growled, his hands already going to her waist. "This will not fix me. It will only make me hungry for more."

"Being hungry for me is never unfortunate, Bjarke." She tilted her head slightly and moved her lips slowly towards his. His growl morphed into a groan as she tasted him. Her lips played over his as her nails gently scraped over his scalp.

The horn blew again. The cacophony of other villagers rushing to the shore was growing louder.

Dalla ended the kiss, pulling back, brushing Bjarke's scarred cheeks with her thumbs. "You are jarl, Bjarke. You must fulfill your duty."

He sighed heavily and nodded. "Aye." He pressed a kiss to her forehead before releasing his hold on her hips. He took her hand, and they went together towards the shore.

CHAPTER 31

Sokki was by Bjarke's side as he stopped to squint into the sunrise. "Jarl, it is one of our own. We believe it may be your brothers, returning from their raids. Should we ready the warriors just in case it is a trap?"

Bjarke thought for a moment, considering the options, taking in the twenty ships that were sailing towards his shores. Sokki was right, the flags waving were Asar's. He did not think he had enemies. He knew only of Beckby and they hadn't had enough warriors to protect themselves. They would not be attacking. But if it were a ploy, and he were not ready…

"Aye. Call for arms. We cannot be certain who is actually on the ships. And we must be ready if it is not our brothers on board."

Bjarke's hand tightened around Dalla's as he felt her pull away. He gazed down at her and shook his head. "No. You will not fight."

She did not cower. "I will fight. If I do not fight, we may die."

She brushed a hand over her belly, making it clear she was also speaking of the babe. "All of us."

They went together to ready for the ships. When they sailed closer to the shore Bjarke was certain it was his brothers and others from the village. "Dalla, you do know what this means."

"That your brothers are alive?"

"Aye. Sigurd too. And with Sigurd acting as jarl…"

Thorvald and Hedin, his youngest brothers jumped off the ships and shrieked like sirens of the seas.

"What a welcome, brother!" Thorvald grabbed his brother by the shoulder and shook him, his other arm waving to the vast ocean of warriors and townspeople, all armed and ready.

"Stand down," Bjarke ordered. Shields and swords lowered, and the two came further into the crowd as the rest of the crew deboarded from the ships. All around there were cries of happiness from wives, mothers, brothers and children who were happy to see their loved ones again.

"Bjarke," Dalla said, grabbing onto his forearm, "with Sigurd acting as jarl, what does that mean?"

Bjarke smiled down at Dalla and rubbed her chin with his fingers. "That you will marry me."

She was stunned, and when she came back to reality, she shook her head. "No. I have married other husbands. I do not want a fourth."

"Dalla, I am your husband whether you declare it to the Gods or not. I would prefer that you did. I do not want to miss you in Valhalla." When she refused to drop her shield, he dropped to his knees and laid his sword at her feet. He stared up at her, his hands on his knees, a man at his weakest. "Please, Dalla. Profess your love for me before the Gods."

She felt her heart hammering in her chest, her eyes glancing around, but no one was paying attention to them, only to the returned warriors coming off the ships. "Yes, I will, Bjarke. I will marry you. Now get up off your knees, your brothers are coming this way."

Bjarke hugged her legs before standing, sword in hand. He was beaming as his two younger brothers came closer into view. They hugged, slapping each other's backs in relief that they had been fortunate enough to return.

"Where are the rest of the ships? You left with fifty." Bjarke stepped back and crossed his arms over his chest as his eyes swept the remaining twenty.

"The seas were not kind, brother. Aegir, the God of the sea, was not in good spirits." Thorvald said, his eyes sweeping over Dalla who stood nearby.

Bjarke turned and nodded to Dalla. She slowly stepped forward to join them. Thorvald raised a brow and Hedin did little to hide his amusement.

Dalla nodded to each of them. "Praise the Gods for your safe return."

"Aye," Hedin replied. "Praise the Gods that you and Bjarke returned in one piece on your raid as well. Asar would be a little duller without the Black Widow wandering about."

"She is no longer the Black Widow, brother. She is my wife."

Thorvald choked back a cough. "Your wife?"

"Aye. His second wife," Dalla interjected, her chin raised defiantly.

Hedin's brow rose with surprise. "Much has happened in our absence, brother."

Thorvald nodded. "Aye. I wonder what else has happened."

"This moon you will hear many tales and we will feast in the fallen's honor. Come, I have much to tell you both." He wrapped his arms around both of their necks and led them towards the Great Hall, Dalla walking beside them. "Where is Sigurd?"

Hedin looked behind them and grinned. "He is entertaining himself already."

Bjarke glanced back and grunted. His brother was walking hand in hand with a maiden. "He will not be pleased with what I must tell him."

"What will you tell him, brother?" Hedin inquired.

"Mother, Father and Kerra were murdered and avenged. I have been acting as jarl in Sigurd's absence, but he must be the one. Our alliances grow weaker, other townships are looking to dethrone the King."

"Harvard?" Thorvald said, disbelief in his voice.

"Aye. He will need to put the maidens aside and make some hard decisions."

"Would you not want to continue as jarl?"

Bjarke shook his head. "If I must, when it is my time. Come, we will speak more of this later. For now let us fill your cups with mead and find you both distractions."

SIGURD'S RISE

"Sigurd, hurry. You are jarl now, you cannot miss the ceremony," his little brother Hedin prodded.

"Aye, you need not remind me repeatedly like one of those terrible mockingbirds. I am well aware of my station, brother."

"I hope that if I tell you often enough I will start to believe it." Hedin chuckled. He slapped Sigurd once on the back and then departed.

Once he was alone Sigurd let out a deep sigh. He had not expected to arrive home and have to take the place of his father. He had expected to be drunk and merry upon his return, his mind free to wander and dream about the adventures he still wished to embark on. That was taken from him now, a thing of the past.

He moved out of his quarters which were tucked against the back corner of the Great Hall and lifted his chin in greeting as he passed by several familiar faces. He winced as the setting sun hit him in the eyes. After a moment he continued, making his way to the water where the ceremony would be held. He was happy for his brother, and at the same time he was concerned. He'd taken the story Bjarke had shared with him to heart. The Seer's message still resounded in his thoughts.

> The Bear and his cub are followed by a Raven. The
> Raven will bring nothing but pain and suffering.
> He must stay away from the Raven and have it
> killed lest it kill him and those he loves.

His brother would swear that Dalla's estranged brother was the raven. But Sigurd was not so sure especially after he'd payed a visit to the Seer himself. The Seer had given the same prophecy and nothing more.

Sigurd forced a smile as he approached the shore. He was just in time to see Bjarke step into the frigid waters to claim his bride who'd been paddled in from her maiden's tent. Villagers cheered as he scooped his wife, covered head to toe in bleached linens, up into his strong arms.

Sigurd's eyes could not help but be locked on Dalla, his brother's bride. Was she indeed the Raven? Could she be trusted? She was not born of Asar. She had never mentioned a brother. What other secrets was she hiding?

Bjarke set down his happy bride, and they each took up their swords. The priestess commenced the ceremony, speaking loudly so that all around them could hear. The villagers were all smiles, excited, Sigurd guessed, by the three-day feast that was to follow.

"Bjarke," she said, "Do you swear to the Gods that this is the woman you wish to marry?"

Bjarke's blue eyes stared into his brides. He nodded. "Aye. I swear to the Gods that there is no other woman in this life that I would have as a wife. There is only her, my shield-maiden, for as long as she will have me."

The priestess nodded her approval and turned her face to Dalla. "And do you Dalla, swear to the Gods that this man is who you wish to marry?"

She nodded, her breath escaping her with a chuckle. "I swear to them."

The priestess nodded and presented the rings, shining bands from the treasures Bjarke and Dalla had acquired their last raid together. "Place the rings on each other. Let them be seen by the Gods, a reminder to them and each other of your love."

After exchanging rings Bjarke wasted no time in grasping his bride, swinging her backwards and kissing her publicly. Sigurd clapped, joining in the crowd. He felt a burning in his chest, whether it was envy or foreboding he could not be sure. But he was sure of one thing at that moment, his brother and his bride had never looked happier.

**MEANWHILE
IN TRELLEBORG...**

King Harvard sat on his throne and regarded the women that sat all around him. He smiled at each and every one. Pleased that they could contain their joy upon having his eyes on them. He had done well choosing his bride and his concubines. They were all maidens of good stock. They knew how to behave. The youngest of them was still learning, but he had no doubt she would soon settle down into the role of a woman.

The doors to his castle opened and Eric, the commander of his armies, came forth and knelt in front of his throne.

"Aye, Eric, why have you come?"

"It displeases me, King Harvard, to report that there is speak of an uprising against you."

King Harvard narrowed his eyes. "How do we know this is not a false accusation?"

"We have the source. She came to us."

"She?" King Harvard's eyebrow raised with curiosity. "Where is this maiden?"

Eric looked down the long aisle before turning back. "She is just outside."

He sighed deeply and clasped his hands against his enlarged belly. "Bring her to me."

Eric stood and marched down the aisle. After a short time he returned, a woman on his hand, her cheeks freshly scarred, her red hair shorter in the front of her skull, but quickly regaining its length.

She bowed down as she reached his feet and began to cry.

King Harvard rolled his eyes towards the Gods and cleared his throat as he motioned for Eric to pick her up.

Eric roughly grabbed her and shook her until she was gazing at the King.

"Do you cry because it pains you think of yourself sitting

before the king? Or do you cry because you know the Gods will punish you for lying to your king?"

She shook her head and bowed it. "No, King Harvard. I cry because I have never seen such a strong, powerful man. And it pains me to think of what will become of you."

He chuckled and rubbed at his long white beard. "Aye? Tell me what you know and where you come from, woman."

Her voice rang clear despite the sniffles of her nose. "I come from Asar, King Harvard. I was married to the jarl there, Jarl Bjarke Marsson. I fled because he found out that I was conspiring to get a message to you, my king. He scarred me and made up lies. But it was well worth the cost to be able to be here before you and deliver the news myself. Please, heed my words, my king. They are coming for your crown."

"Who exactly? Asar's warriors?"

"No. All of them. The jarls. Hraun, Fjall, Gnupar, Beckby and Asar."

The king studied the subject bowed before him and considered her words. "You are thick with child. You will be kept in the south wing. If what you say is untrue I will have your child slaughtered and fed to you. And then I will murder you." With a flick of his fingers he had her carried away.

When it was once again quiet in the hall he stroked his beard. Could it be true? Could the jarls be revolting against him? Yes, he supposed it was. He had stolen most of their women. But he had considered it a sacrifice and a gift. Perhaps they needed reminding of who they owed their prosperity to.

Thank you so much for reading Book 1 in the Nordic Sons Series. I hope you enjoyed the rocky, passionate journey of Dalla and Bjarke and that you fell in love with them as much as I did.

The story is just beginning and I hope you'll pick up the next book in the Nordic Sons series, His Viking Thrall.

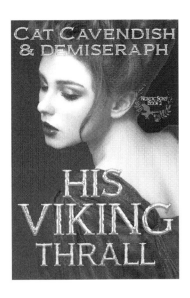

Want to keep up with new releases? Sign up for my (very rare) newsletter:
NEWSLETTER SIGNUP

EXTRAS

While doing research for this book I stumbled upon quite a few great resources.

The inspiration for this book was, of course, History Channel's show, Vikings starring Travis Fimmel and Katheryne Winnick. The choppy way my Vikings speak is attributed to them. If you want to get more in the spirit of Vikings and experience more of their culture and beliefs while also being entertained I would highly recommend checking out the show.

Music I was inspired by was by an artist named Danheim. With headphones on I could feel the beats and the power I imagine he is trying to convey through his music. Check them out with Amazon's Music Prime, on Spotify or Youtube.

Web Resources for Viking Research:

http://www.history.com/news/10-things-you-may-not-know-about-the-vikings

https://www.historychannel.com.au/articles/viking-life-and-customs/

http://www.bbc.co.uk/history/ancient/vikings/religion_01.shtml

https://www.visitnorway.com/things-to-do/art-culture/vikings/

https://www.historyonthenet.com/viking-law-and-government-the-thing/

http://thenorsegods.com/the-norse-gods/

Printed in Great Britain
by Amazon